Praise for Richard Stark and the Parker novels:

"Super-ingenious, super-lethal. . . . Parker is super-tough."
—*New York Times Book Review*

"Westlake's ability to construct an action story filled with unforeseen twists and quadruple-crosses is unparalleled."
—*San Francisco Chronicle*

"Parker is a brilliant invention. . . . What chiefly distinguishes Westlake, under whatever name, is his passion for process and mechanics. . . . Parker appears to have eliminated everything from his program but machine logic, but this is merely protective coloration. He is a romantic vestige, a free-market anarchist whose independent status is becoming a thing of the past."
—Luc Sante, *The New York Review of Books*

"Richard Stark's Parker . . . is refreshingly amoral, a thief who always gets away with the swag."
—Stephen King, *Entertainment Weekly*

"Elmore Leonard wouldn't write what he does if Stark hadn't been there before. And Quentin Tarantino wouldn't write what he does without Leonard. . . . Old master that he is, Stark does them all one better."
—*L.A. Times*

"Westlake is among the smoothest, most engaging writers on the planet."
San Diego Tribune

T0043249

The Jugger

RICHARD STARK

With a New Foreword by John Banville

The University of Chicago Press

The University of Chicago Press, Chicago 60637
© 1965 by Richard Stark
Foreword © 2009 by John Banville
All rights reserved.
First published in 1965 by Pocket Books. Reprinted in 2002 by
Mysterious Press.
University of Chicago Press edition 2009

Printed in the United States of America

15 14 13 12 11 10 09   1 2 3 4 5

ISBN-13: 978-0-226-77102-1 (paper)
ISBN-10: 0-226-77102-4 (paper)

Library of Congress Cataloging-in-Publication Data

Stark, Richard, 1933–
    The jugger / Richard Stark ; with a new foreword by John Banville.
        p. cm.
    Summary: A Parker novel, which has the main character in Sagamore,
Nebraska, at the request of Joe Sheer, a retired safe cracker who carries
many of Parker's criminal secrets.
    ISBN-13: 978-0-226-77102-1 (pbk. : alk. paper)
    ISBN-10: 0-226-77102-4 (pbk. : alk. paper)   1. Parker (Fictitious
character).   I. Banville, John.   II. Title.
    PS3573.E9J84   2009
    813'.54—dc22

                                                    2008042432

♾ The paper used in this publication meets the minimum require-
ments of the American National Standard for Information Sciences—
Permanence of Paper for Printed Library Materials, ANSI Z39.48-1992.

THE PARKER NOVELS
John Banville

It was in the 1960s that Richard Stark began writing his masterly series of Parker novels—at last count there were twenty-four of them—but they are as unrepresentative of the Age of Aquarius as it is possible to be. Try imagining this most hardened of hard-boiled criminals in a tie-dyed shirt and velvet bell-bottoms. Parker does not do drugs, having no interest in expanding his mind or deepening his sensibilities; he cares nothing for politics and is indifferent to foreign wars, although he fought or at least took part in one of them; he would rather make money than love and would be willing to give peace a chance provided he could sneak round the back of the love-in and rob everybody's unattended stuff. When he goes to San Francisco it is not to leave his heart there—has Parker got a heart?—but to retrieve some money the Outfit owes him and kill a lot of people in the process.

The appeal of the conventional crime novel is the sense of completion it offers. Life is a mess—we do not remember being born, and death, as Ludwig Wittgenstein wisely observed, is not an experience in life, so that all we have is a chaotic middle, bristling with loose ends, in which nothing is ever properly over and done with. It could be said, of course, that all fiction of whatever genre offers a beginning, middle, and end—even *Finnegans Wake* has a shape—but crime fiction does it best of all. No matter how unlikely the cast of suspects or how baffling the strew of clues in an Agatha Christie whodunit or a Robert Ludlum thriller, we know with a certainty not afforded by real life that when the murderer is unmasked or the conspiracy foiled, everything will click into place, like a jigsaw puzzle assembling itself before our eyes. The Parker books, however, take it as a given that if something can go wrong, it will, and that since something always can go wrong, it invariably does.

Indeed, this is how very many of the Parker stories begin, with things going or gone disastrously awry. And Parker is at his most inventive when at his most desperate.

We first encountered Parker in *The Hunter,* published in 1962. His creator, Donald Westlake, was already an established writer—he adopted the pen name Richard Stark because, as he said in a recent interview, "When you're first in love, you want to do it all the time," and in the early days he was writing so much and so often that he feared the Westlake market would soon become glutted.

Born in 1933, Westlake is indeed a protean writer and, like Parker, the complete professional. Besides crime novels, he has written short stories, comedies, science fiction, and screenplays—his tough, elegant screenplay for *The Grifters,* adapted from a Jim Thompson novel, was nominated for an Academy Award. Surely the finest movie he wrote, however, is *Point Blank,* a noir masterpiece based on the first Parker novel, *The Hunter,* directed by John Boorman and starring Lee Marvin. Anyone who saw the film will consider Marvin the quintessential Parker, though Westlake has said that when he first created his relentless hero—hero?—he imagined him looking more like Jack Palance.

In that first book, *The Hunter,* Parker was a rough diamond—"I'd done nothing to make him easy for the reader," says Westlake, "no small talk, no quirks, no pets" —and looked like a classic pulp fiction hoodlum:

> He was big and shaggy, with flat square shoulders and arms too long in sleeves too short. . . . His hands, swinging curve-fingered at his sides, looked like they were molded of brown clay by a sculptor who thought big and liked veins. His hair was brown and dry and dead, blowing around his head like a poor toupee about to fly loose. His face was a chipped chunk of concrete, with eyes of flawed onyx. His mouth was a quick stroke, bloodless. (p. 3–4)

Even before the end of this short book, however, we see Westlake/Stark begin to cut and burnish his brand-new creation, giving him facets and sharp angles and flashes of a hard, inner fire. He has been betrayed by his best friend and shot by his wife, and now he is owed money by the Outfit—the Mafia, we assume—and he is not going to stop until he has been repaid:

Momentum kept him rolling. He wasn't sure himself any more how much was a tough front to impress the organization and how much was himself. He knew he was hard, he knew that he worried less about emotion than other people. But he'd never enjoyed the idea of a killing. . . . It was momentum, that was all. Eighteen years in one business, doing one or two clean fast simple operations a year, living relaxed and easy in the resort hotels the rest of the time with a woman he liked, and then all of a sudden it all got twisted around. The woman was gone, the pattern was gone, the relaxation was gone, the clean swiftness was gone. (p. 171)

The fact is, though Parker himself would be contemptuous of the notion, he is the perfection of that existential man whose earliest models we met in Nietzsche and Kierkegaard and Dostoevsky. If Parker has ever read Goethe—and perhaps he has?—he will have recognized his own natural motto in Faust's heaven-defying declaration: "*Im Anfang war die Tat*" [In the beginning was the deed]. Donald Westlake puts it in more homely terms when he says that, "I've always believed the books are really about a workman at work, doing the work to the best of his ability," and when in the context of Parker he refers to "Hemingway's judgment on people, that the competent guy does it on his own and the incompetents lean on each other."

In Parker's world there is no law, unless it is the law of the quick and the merciless against the dim and the slow. The police never appear, or if they do they are always too late to stop Parker doing what he is intent on doing. Only twice has he been caught and—briefly—jailed, once after the betrayal by his wife and Mal Resnick, which sets *The Hunter* in vengeful motion, and another time in the recent *Breakout*. Parker treats the law-abiding world, that tame world where most of us live, with tight-lipped impatience or, when one or other of us is unfortunate enough to stumble into his path and hinder him, with lethal efficiency. Significantly, it is the *idea* of a killing that he has never enjoyed; this is not to say that he would enjoy the killing itself, but that he regards the necessity of murder as a waste of essential energies, energies that would be better employed elsewhere.

Violence in the Parker books is always quick and clean and all the more shocking in its swiftness and cleanliness. In one of the books—it would be a spoiler to specify which—Parker forces a young man to dig a hole in the dirt floor of a cellar in search of something buried there, and when the thing has been found, the scene closes with a brief, bald line informing us that Parker shot the young fellow and buried him in the hole he had dug. In another story, Parker and one of his crew tie a hoodlum to a chair and torture some vital information out of him, after which they lock him in a closet, still chairbound, and depart, indifferent to the fact that no one knows where the hoodlum is and so there will be no one to free him.

With the exception of the likes of James M. Cain, Jim Thompson, and Georges Simenon—that is, the Simenon not of the Maigret books but of what he called his *romans durs*, his hard novels—all crime writers are sentimentalists at heart, even, or especially, when they are at their bloodiest. In conventional tales of murder, mayhem, and the fight for right, what the reader is offered is escape, if only into the dream of a world where men are men and women love them for it, where crooks are crooks and easily identified by the scars on their faces and the Glocks in their fists, where policemen are dull but honest and usually dealing with a bad divorce, where a good man is feared by the lawless and respected by the law-abiding: in short, where life is otherwise and better. In the Parker books, however, it is the sense of awful and immediate reality that makes them so startling, so unsettling, and so convincing.

As the series goes on, Parker has become more intricate in motivation and more polished in manner—his woman, Claire, the replacement for his wife Lynn, the one who shot him and subsequently committed suicide, is a fascinating creation, forbearing, loving, nurturing, the perfect companion for a professional—yet in more than forty years his creator has never allowed him to weaken or to mellow. The most recent caper, *Dirty Money,* published in 2008, ends with a vintage exchange between Parker, a woman, and a grifter who was foolish enough to try pulling a fast one on Parker:

> He helped McWhitney to lie back on the bed, then said to Sandra, "If we do this right, you can get me to Claire's place by two in the morning."
>
> "What a good person I am," she said.
>
> "If you leave me here," the guy on the floor said, "he'll kill me tomorrow morning."
>
> Parker looked at him. "So you've still got tonight," he said.

And that is about as much as Parker, or Richard Stark, is ever willing to allow to anyone.

The Jugger

PART ONE

PART ONE

1

When the knock came at the door, Parker was just turning to the obituary page. He put the paper down and looked around the room, and everything was clean and ordinary. He walked over and opened the door.

The little guy standing there was dressed like he was kidding around. Dark green trousers, black-and-white shoes, orange shirt with black string tie, tweed sport jacket with leather elbow patches. The fluffy corners of a lavender handkerchief peeped up from his jacket pocket. His left hand was negligently tucked into his trouser pocket, and his right hand was stuck inside his jacket like an imitation of Napoleon. He had the lined and leathery weasel face of an alky or a tout, and he was both. He was somewhere past forty, short of eighty.

He grinned, showing big bad teeth, and said, "Parker, you're an ugly man. You're uglier with the new face, and that's a wonder."

Parker recognized him. His name was Tiftus and he

claimed to be a lock man. Parker had never worked with him because he was too unreliable.

Tiftus grinned some more and said, "Invite me in, why don't you? We've got talk to do."

It couldn't be coincidence; this had to be something to do with Joe Sheer. But Parker, to make sure, said, "About what? What talk would we have?"

"Not in the hall, Parker. Where's your manners?"

"Go to hell."

Tiftus kept on grinning. He shook his head and withdrew his right hand from his jacket far enough for Parker to see the silver sparkle of a Hi-Standard .25-caliber automatic. "Be nice," he said. "We have a nice talk about old times. And old friends."

So it was about Joe. Parker stepped back and motioned for Tiftus to come in. Smug as a peacock, Tiftus stepped over the threshold and into Parker's right hand. Parker chopped him midway between belt buckle and automatic, and Tiftus' face turned from tan leather to grey elephant skin. Parker plucked the automatic from his hand, yanked him farther into the room, and shut the door.

Tiftus was making a sound in his throat like an air-raid siren heard from far away. Parker pushed him into the room's one armchair, and went over to the window to look out. Captain Younger was still down there under his cowboy hat, leaning against the fender of his black Ford in the September sunlight. Across the way was the railroad station. Sagamore, Nebraska. The few cars going by on the main street were dusty in the sunlight.

No one else seemed to be hanging around, not outside. If Tiftus had anyone with him, they were either in the lobby downstairs or waiting for him out of sight somewhere.

Parker put the little automatic in the drawer of the writing table and looked over at Tiftus, but he was still sitting ramrod-straight in the chair, forearms clamped to his belly, the air-raid siren still keening far away in the back of his throat.

Parker took the time to finish looking at the paper. He'd already opened it to the obituaries. He looked down the list, and found it, under Joe's alias:

SHARDIN—Joseph T., Sept. 17, no living relations. Funeral Wednesday 10 a.m. Bernard Gliffe Funeral Chapel, Interment Greenlawn Cemetery.

Wednesday; today. Ten a.m. He looked at his watch, and it was after eleven now, so the funeral was probably over. It wouldn't have taken long, with nobody there who knew Joe.

He turned back to the first page and went through the paper completely, reading all the headlines, looking for some reference to the way Joe died, but there was no mention of Joe at all except the obituary notice. The notice didn't say what Joe died of.

There was a photo on page seven of Captain Abner L. Younger and three other stocky types at a Safety

First Conference, figuring out how to keep the school-children from being killed by bad drivers. The cowboy hat made it tough to see Younger's eyes.

Parker closed the paper finally and went over to stand in front of Tiftus, who was now breathing again. Tiftus' face had changed color one more time, now being flat white all over except for pained brown eyes and two round red spots of color on leathery cheeks, looking like rouge painted on there to make him look like a clown. He was breathing with his mouth open, and watching Parker with his pained eyes, but he didn't say anything. The bright clothing looked even more out of place than it had before.

Parker said, "You want to talk. Talk."

Tiftus moved his lips, but he didn't say anything. Then he closed his mouth, and swallowed noisily, and licked his tongue across his dry lips, and finally he did talk, saying, "You didn't have to do that." His voice sounded rusty. "I almost threw up," he said. He sounded offended.

Parker said, "How old are you, Tiftus? A hundred? You don't know about guns, at your age? Don't ever show a gun to a man you don't want to kill. You're a moron, Tiftus. Now, what did you want to talk about?"

"Not with you, you bastard." Parker had hurt his feelings, and he was going to pout.

Parker said, "What did Joe die of?"

Tiftus seemed honestly surprised; so surprised, anyway, he forgot about pouting. He said, "What the hell? How should I know?"

"Weren't you here?"

"Who, me?"

Parker shook his head, irritated. He rapped Tiftus' chest with a knuckle, and Tiftus winced. He rapped again and said, "Don't ask questions. I ask you a question, what you do next you answer it, you don't ask another question. You ready to try again?"

"You don't have to do like this, Parker. I just come around here friendly, so I figure we . . ."

"With a toy gun."

"All right. All right, you're right, I apologize about that." He was recovering at last, coming back up to be the chipper bantam again. "I shouldn't have flashed the gun on you that way."

"I already knew that. Tell me something I don't know."

Tiftus spread his hands in a gesture of peace. "We've got no reason to fight each other, Parker," he said. "We've never been enemies, never in our lives. There's never been any bad blood between us at all."

"There's never been anything between us. When did you get to town here?"

"Just now. What do you think, for Christ's sake? Parker, I haven't even unpacked yet. I got off the train, I came across the street, I saw you coming into the hotel, I got your room number from the desk clerk, that's all. I got a room, one floor up, left my suitcase there and came right down to see you. Why should we work against each other?"

"Why should we work with each other?"

Tiftus was getting sure of himself again, smug again. "Because we're both here," he said. "We're both after the same thing."

"We are? What's that?"

But Tiftus smirked and waggled a finger and got coy. "You know as well as I do, Parker. You want to find out how much I know, is that it?"

What Parker wanted to find out was what the hell Tiftus thought he was talking about. But he couldn't let Tiftus guess he didn't know, so he'd have to fake it and wait for Tiftus to let something slip.

He said, "I don't give a damn what you know. I still don't see any reason to put in with you. I'd never work with you before this because you can't be counted on, and I'm not going to work with you now."

"Ah, but this is different," Tiftus said. "This time you *can* count on me. You can count on me to be right here in this monotonous little town right down to the finish. *You're* here, and *I'm* here, and neither one of us is leaving. If we fight each other, we'll just draw attention to ourselves. If we work together, we'll be done that much sooner."

Parker didn't bother to tell him about Captain Younger, that attention had already been drawn. Instead, he said, "What if I told you I don't know what the hell you're talking about?"

Tiftus laughed and looked cunning and said, "Oh, come on, Parker! What are you *doing* here, then? I suppose you're here for your health, or you just thought you'd come by for Joe's funeral, is that it?"

Parker considered. Tiftus was stupid in some ways, but clever in others; it wasn't likely he'd tell Parker more than he'd already told. But if Parker kept poking around asking more questions, Tiftus would begin to believe he really didn't know the story after all, and that would be no good.

Parker leaned forward, his left arm straight out, hand resting on the back of the armchair by Tiftus' head. Lowering his voice, he said, "All right, Tiftus, I'll tell you the truth. I'll tell you why I'm really here."

Tiftus cocked his head, the better to listen.

Parker clubbed him across the side of the jaw. Tiftus' head snapped over and bounced off Parker's left forearm. He sagged forward and would have fallen out of the chair, but Parker pushed him back.

Parker went through his pockets. Nothing in the jacket at all but that lavender handkerchief, which turned out to be scented. In the pocket of the orange shirt was an unopened five-pack of plastic-tipped little cigars. In the right-hand trouser pocket was a Zippo lighter inscribed FROM DW TO SF, neither set of initials having any connection with Tiftus. In the left-hand trouser pocket were fifty-seven cents in change, his hotel room key, and a rabbit's foot. In his hip pocket was his wallet, and in the wallet were a Social Security card made out to Adolph Tiftus, a Nevada driver's license, four black-and-white photographs of horses, a photo of Tiftus himself from a coin-operated photo booth, sixty-four dollars in bills, a clipping from a *Daily Telegraph* column that mentioned his name as present at the opening of Freehold Raceway one prewar season, a small torn-off piece of adding-machine paper with two telephone numbers written on it in pencil, and an obscene photograph in color of a Chinese couple standing up.

Nothing in pockets or wallet told him what Tiftus was doing in Sagamore, Nebraska, a useless town forty miles from Omaha. The telephone numbers were not the Sagamore exchange. There was no race track in the vicinity. Joe Sheer hadn't had anything to do with race tracks, except to hit them maybe sometimes. Joe had never been a gambler of any kind; that was why he was so good, before he retired.

Parker put everything back in Tiftus' pockets except the room key. He picked Tiftus up like a ventriloquist picking up his dummy, threw him over his shoulder, and went over to the hall door.

There was no one in sight in the hall. Parker took the time to go back across the room and get Tiftus' gun out of the dresser and stuff it in his pocket. Then he went out to the hall, locked the room door, and went down towards the red light that showed him where the staircase was.

Tiftus was all bones and leather flesh, as light as a tick. Parker carried him up the one flight and down another deserted hallway, and used Tiftus' key to open the door.

Tiftus hadn't been lying. His suitcase, closed and full, sat on the bed. A camel's hair topcoat, getting a little seedy at collar and cuffs and bottom edge, was sprawled across the armchair in a debonair manner. Tiftus had divested himself of these two things and gone right on down to Parker's room.

Parker went over and dumped Tiftus on his back on the bed. He heard a sound just as he let Tiftus go, and turned. The connecting door to the next room had opened. A woman was standing there in the doorway, wearing a white hotel robe on her left forearm and pink, puffy slippers on her feet and nothing else. She was yellow above, black below, and she'd been out in the sun for a tan while wearing a two-piece bathing suit. She was built heavy but not fat; firm flesh well padded over a big-boned frame. Her face would have been beautiful except that she had the eyes of a pickpocket and the mouth of a whore.

She said, "What the hell are you doing?"

So Tiftus had left three things behind before coming to see Parker: bag, coat, and bag. The other bag had been stashed in an adjoining room to take itself a shower. Parker said, "Go back in there and keep your mouth shut."

"Says you. What happened to my man?"

"Your what?"

"Never mind, you. He's little but he's wiry." And about twice her age, if she was the thirty she looked.

Parker said, "I'm the one he had business with. Beat it."

As an afterthought, she held the towel up in front of herself. Now she looked like a calendar in a firehouse.

She said, "Not till I find out what happened to poor Adolph."

"He fell over an ambition."

"Is that supposed to be funny?"

Parker walked over and put his hand on the middle of the towel and pushed. He shut the connecting door and threw the bolt lock, then went back over to the bed. The woman rapped on the door a few times, but quit when Parker ignored her. He knew she'd have more sense than to holler for the law or anything like that; connected up with Tiftus, she'd have to know that much.

He took Tiftus' suitcase off the bed, out from under one of Tiftus' sprawled legs, and put it on top of the dresser and opened it. He threw clothing out piece by piece, it all piling up on the floor beside him, but when he was done all he had was an empty suitcase and a lot of junk lying around on the floor. Clothing, toothpaste and toothbrush, tube of zinc ointment, tube of some sort of cream for piles, more obscene photographs of the same bored Chinese couple, box of cartridges for the automatic, hair oil, three astrology magazines. Still nothing to let him know Tiftus' game.

Ask the woman? No, even Tiftus should know enough to keep his business to himself. The woman would be along for after work, not during.

Then wait around for Tiftus to come out of it, and ask him direct? No, the hell with it for now. There wasn't much time, and Tiftus shouldn't be allowed to find out how little Parker knew.

Parker dropped the room key in the empty suitcase and went over to the door. He stopped there to look back, but Tiftus was still out. There was no sound from the woman in the next room. Parker left, closing the door carefully behind himself.

Down to the right were the elevator and the stairs he'd come up just now, but there ought to be a fire exit the other way, one that wouldn't lead to the lobby or any part of the front of the building. Parker went off in that direction and found it right around the first turn, a broad wooden door with FIRE EXIT on it in red letters. It opened rustily, reluctantly. Parker came out onto an exterior staircase running down the clapboard back of the building, an old, wide, wooden fire escape with age-warped banisters. He went down it to a little concrete alley lined with green doors and garbage cans. At the end of it was the street.

Parker stood looking out at the street for a minute before leaving the alley. He didn't see Captain Younger, nor anybody who looked offhand as though he might be working for Captain Younger. Nor anybody who looked as though he might be linked up with Tiftus; though on that score Parker was pretty sure Tiftus was working alone. If there were a second man with him, anyone besides the woman, Parker would have seen some sort of evidence of him by now.

He left the alley and started down the street towards a drugstore on the next corner. He remembered the name from the obituary; in the drugstore he'd get the address and the directions for getting there.

2

The room stank of flowers and death. Orange light-bulbs shaped like wrinkled mosques shone dimly in wall fixtures on the left, gleaming on the tangled pattern of the wallpaper, muting and deadening in the thick maroon rug and the heavy dark draperies around the doorways. To the right, rotting flowers in green wicker baskets stood around a coffinless bier; a few white rose petals had fallen onto the flat tabletop of the bier and were slowly browning and curling into tiny fists.

Parker stood in the main entrance a minute, getting used to the dimness after the bright sunshine of the street. The room was hollow, muffled, empty of people, with no one standing next to the door near the podium containing the book for visitors to sign, and no one sitting on the maroon mohair sofas in the corner alcoves.

Parker shut the front door and started across the

room, his passage making no sound at all on the thick carpet.

Going through the curtained doorway at the far end of the room was like time travel, like leaping across the years out of the muffled darkness of the Victorian era and into the plane geometry of the age of IBM. The walls of this corridor, painted grey, looked like some sort of spackled plastic in a poor imitation of stucco; the ceiling was a gridwork of white sound-proofing panels with small black holes in rows; and the floor was black composition that deadened the sound of Parker's feet almost as much as the maroon rug had in the other room.

Midway along the corridor two white doors faced one another. Parker tried the one on the left and saw a flight of stairs leading down to darkness. The door on the right was better; it led to a small office done in the same IBM style as the corridor, but with old-fashioned glass-fronted bookcases flanking the window.

The office, too, was empty. Parker stepped through the doorway and looked around. There was no paper in the electric typewriter on the side desk, nothing disrupting the bare neatness of the main desk, no coat or hat on the coatrack in the corner. The place looked like a fake office in some furniture company's display room.

He turned around to go back out to the hall, and the doorway was suddenly filled by a chunky aggrieved-looking type in a tight black suit, a chauffeur's cap, and grey cloth gloves. He stared at Parker from under bunched eyebrows and said, "What you doing in there?"

"Looking for Gliffe."

"What?"

"Bernard Gliffe. He runs this place, he's your boss."

"I know who Mr. Gliffe is."

"You know where he is?"

He still looked aggrieved, but not at Parker, more as though it was his normal expression, as though the injustice that had been done him had cut so deep he'd never lose the scar, even though it had happened so long ago, he couldn't really remember what it was anymore. He nodded and said, "Sure I know where he is."

"Where?"

"Upstairs taking his nap."

"His what?"

"Whenever we got a morning job out to Greenlawn, he takes a nap afterwards. You want him for something special?"

Parker said, "I want to talk to him about Joseph Shardin."

"Who?"

"You buried him this morning," Parker told him. "He was the morning job out to Greenlawn."

"Oh. Oh, him." He shook his head. "I never know the name of the stiffs," he said. "Unless it's my own family or something, that's different."

"You want to get Gliffe?"

"Yeah, okay. You can't wait in there, you got to wait out in the viewing-room."

"The what?"

He meant the room Parker had already gone through, with the flowers and the bier. Parker waited in there five minutes, pacing up and down on the maroon carpet. He wondered if Tiftus was awake yet, if Captain Younger had discovered yet that Parker was no longer in the hotel. He didn't know how much time he had.

Gliffe at last came through the draperies at the far end of the room, like an apologetic Sydney Greenstreet. He was an extremely tall, somewhat heavy-set man, with sloping shoulders and broad beam and flat-footed stance. He was about fifty, black hair turning grey at the temples the way it was supposed to, face pallid as bread dough and jowly as a squirrel. His eyes were pale blue, watery, slightly protuberant beneath skimpy eyebrows; at the moment they were blinking away sleep. He was wearing a black suit and black tie.

He came forward as improbably light as a Macy's parade balloon, his dead-fish hand extended. "I am Bernard Gliffe," he said. "You are . . ."

For Gliffe, Parker put on his businessman face. He shook Gliffe's hand and said, "Willis. Charles Willis." It was the name he'd used before on trips to this town, so he was using it this time, too. The way he said the name, he had to be a businessman of some kind. The way he looked, big and square and hard, it had to be a tough and competitive business; used cars maybe, or jukeboxes.

Gliffe said, "A friend of Mr. Shardin's, Benny tells

me." His eyes glittered just a little when he said Joe's name.

Parker said, "That's right. That's why I'm here."

"Come into the office. We can sit down and chat."

The chauffeur—Benny, apparently—was nowhere in sight. Parker followed Gliffe down the hall and back into the office, and Gliffe eased around and settled into the chair behind the main desk like a dirigible mooring. Parker sat in the client chair behind the desk.

Gliffe said, "A sad thing about Mr. Shardin. Sad indeed." It was just words, a conversation-filler.

Parker said, "The paper didn't have much to say about how he died."

"A heart attack, I believe. You knew Mr. Shardin well?" Again there was that touch of excitement in his eyes, quickly covered.

"Since before he retired," Parker said.

"Ah." Gliffe nodded solemnly, eyes hooded, and formed a little tent with his hands on the desk, fingertips together. "I never met Mr. Shardin in life," he said. "A recent resident in our community." His tone was supposed to inspire confidence, information.

But information was what Parker wanted. He said, "You never knew him?"

"No, I'm sorry to say I did not. A very pleasant and agreeable man, from all accounts."

"How come you got the job?"

Gliffe looked slightly offended for just a second, but then it was gone and he said, "As there were no known living relatives, it fell upon the municipality to make the arrangements for burial, and the assignment de- volved upon me." He spread his hands as though to say that death is terrible but inevitable and someone must perform these sad duties. Then he brightened and said, "Do you come from Mr. Shardin's home town?"

"No, we were in the same business awhile. Who's handling the estate?"

"The Citizen's Trust, I believe. Yes, Citizen's Trust. Mr. Shardin had an account there and, as he died in- testate, the court appointed the bank executor. So you were both in the same business, eh?"

"For a while." Gliffe's attempts to pump for infor- mation were surprising in their strength. Parker, brushing them off, still wondered about them; Gliffe shouldn't be that interested in someone he'd never known alive.

Before Gliffe could ask his next question, Parker said, "Who was his doctor?"

"His doctor?" Gliffe seemed puzzled. "I believe it was Dr. Rayborn. Why, what makes you ask?"

"I thought I might go see him. I'd been out of touch with Joe; I'd like to know what happened to him."

"Well, of course, age must come to us all eventually, and Mr. Shardin was not a young man; seventy-one years of age, I believe."

"Something like that."

"He had led a full life," he said, as though all that Joe's life had lacked till now was Gliffe's mouthing this little epitaph, "and, I trust, a happy one. But you would know more about that than I."

"He had a happy life. Where is this Dr. Rayborn?"

"His office is just a block from here, west on Lake Avenue. Though, to be perfectly frank with you, Mr. Willis, I don't understand your desire to see him. Mr. Shardin is gone; nothing any of us can do will bring him back."

"I don't want to bring him back. I want to hear about how he died."

"Surely you have no suspicion there was anything untoward in Mr. Shardin's death?"

But Parker shook his head. "I know he had a bad heart," he said, lying. "That was why he retired when he did. I don't think there's anything funny about the way he died; who'd want to kill him or do him any harm? He was just an old guy, retired, taking it easy."

"Certainly." Gliffe nodded, smiling fatuously. "The golden years," he said. "I myself am looking forward—but that, of course, is in the future. What business did you say Mr. Shardin was in?"

So he'd finally come out with the question head-on. In answer to it, Parker said, "He wasn't in any business around here, he was retired."

Before Gliffe could say anything else, explain what he'd meant to say or try to pin Parker down more closely, Parker got to his feet and said, "I better be going. I don't want to take too much of your time."

"Not at all, not at all."

Gliffe stood up behind the desk, his lips pursing just

a trifle in discontent. They shook hands again, and Gliffe said, "I'm happy to have had a chance to meet someone who knew Mr. Shardin in life. Not having had the opportunity to know him, I was frankly curious about him, about his past, his friendships, his life in general."

"Well, that's all over for him now," Parker said.

Irritation flickered across Gliffe's face. "Yes," he said. "So it is."

Parker said, "I can find my own way out."

3

Iiftus was on the lawn, sitting on the sign that said FUNERAL HOME.

He got to his feet when Parker walked out to the sunlight, and came over towards Parker smiling and tapping his head. "Am I smart?" he wanted to know.

Parker said, "No."

"I'm in your room there, you've got the local paper. I says to myself, what the hell does Parker want with a crummy local paper? What else but the obituary, the undertaker's address? Now, am I smart?"

Parker stood in front of him and said, "Already today I hit you twice. Once I knocked the wind out of you, once I knocked the consciousness out of you. Here you are back the third time. You call that smart?"

"I told you you could count on me this time, Parker, and I meant it." The little man was smiling his cocky grin, but underneath it there was steel; something new and different for Tiftus. He said, "If you want us to be partners, that's okay. If you want us to be competitors, that's okay, too. It's up to you."

Parker said, "Good-bye." He started down the street.

But Tiftus hadn't been giving an ultimatum after all. He trailed along, bright as a counterfeit penny, trotting to keep up with Parker's long stride. "You really put a scare into Rhonda," he said, as though it were something funny but slightly naughty Parker had done. "You really scared her."

Rhonda. She must have picked up the name the same place she got the tan.

"We're both in this," Tiftus said, panting a little because of having to move so fast. "Don't think I'll quit."

Parker kept walking, ignoring him.

Tiftus trotted and panted, skipping along in Parker's wake like a Scottish terrier. He said, "Where you going now, Parker? You going out to Joe's house? You know where it is?"

Parker strode on.

Tiftus said, "You been here before, haven't you? You and Joe was good buddies, wasn't you?"

Parker had nothing to say to him.

Tiftus said, "I know it, Parker, I know all about it. You used to come up here and visit him all the time, I heard about that. You think you got the inside track now, don't you?"

Parker said nothing, but he was listening. Tiftus might say something useful after all.

Tiftus said, "I'm not greedy, Parker, you know me, you know I'm not the greedy type. We could work something out. You hear me?"

Parker didn't slacken his pace, but he said, to see if Tiftus would tell him anything, "Work what out?"

"The split," Tiftus said, as though that explained anything. As though it explained everything. "The split." He said it twice. "I don't ask fifty-fifty," he said, and his voice showed he knew how generous he was being. "I know Joe was your friend, you got more of a claim than me, I know that. But I'm here, too, Parker, you got to accept that. I got a claim, too, because I'm here. You got to work out a split with me."

"How much?"

"Make me an offer."

Damn Tiftus! He kept talking all the time, talking as though he knew exactly what he was talking about, but he never said anything. Jabber jabber jabber, and nothing coming out.

Some things were obvious: Tiftus was here because he thought there was money to be made here somewhere, and his hope for money was connected with Joe Sheer somehow, and he figured Parker was here for the same reason. But did Tiftus' hopes and expectations have anything to do with Joe's troubles? Or with the way Joe died? Or with why Captain Younger was hanging around?

There were too many questions, too few answers, and not enough time.

It was too bad Tiftus was such a loser, so unreliable,

such a mistake. If it had been somebody with brains and dependability, somebody like Handy McKay or Salsa, Parker would have worked an arrangement with him by now and they'd all know where they stood. But not Tiftus; Parker wouldn't link up with Tiftus ever.

Take the business of the woman. Tiftus is supposed to be coming here to work, and he brings a woman along. Parker had a woman, too, and he'd left her in Miami when he'd come up here. But Tiftus brought his along; a man who won't give up comfort for success makes a bad partner.

Tiftus said again, "Make me an offer, Parker."

The only thing to do was get away from Tiftus, ignore him, find out what there was to know from other sources. Parker stopped, turned, and grabbed a handful of orange shirt. "Here's the offer," he said. "Third time today."

"Don't!"

Parker clipped him, enough to feel but not enough to knock him out. When he let the little man go, Tiftus sat down on the sidewalk like a baby.

Parker stood over him, hands closed into fists. "The next time you show up," he said, "I'll fix you so you don't show up anymore. You know me, Tiftus, you know I don't say things for fun."

Tiftus didn't say anything. He just sat there.

Parker looked around. They were on a residential street, houses with porches. A few cars went by, and the people in them looked curiously at Parker and Tiftus but didn't stop. There were no pedestrians in this block.

Parker said, "Good-bye, Tiftus."

He turned around and walked away. Behind him, Tiftus just sat on the sidewalk. The people in the cars going by looked at the brightly dressed little man sitting on the sidewalk. After a few minutes he got to his feet and went away. He didn't follow Parker.

4

It looked like a private home, except for the small metal sign on the lawn:

L. D. RAYBORN, MD

Parker went up on the broad porch and saw the other sign beside the front door. This one simply said OFFICE and had an arrow pointing away to the right. Parker went that way, his steps echoing on the bare boards of the porch. The porch was freshly painted but empty of furniture, as though the house were vacant. At the side of the house he saw that the porch went around to a little cubby-hole where there was another door.

And another sign, this one above the doorbell: RING AND WALK IN.

He rang, then tried the knob. The door was locked. Exasperated, he rang again, longer this time.

He was just about to go back to try the main door

when this one opened, and an angry nurse, glaring at him through the screen door, said, "Office hours are not until *two*."

Parker shook his head. "I'm not a patient," he said. "I want to see the doctor on another matter."

"I can't help that," she said. "Office hours are not until two."

"Then I'll try him at home," Parker told her. He turned around and went away, and behind him she called, "It won't do you any good. Office hours are not until *two*."

He went back around the empty porch to the main door and rang the bell, and after a minute the door was opened by a stocky man in paint-smeared trousers and a grey undershirt. "Yes? Can I help you?"

"I'm looking for Dr. Rayborn."

"That's me, oddly enough," the stocky man said, and smiled down at the clothes he was wearing. "I've just been puttering around." He was about fifty, with a sort of professional joviality about him, but not bad enough to be offensive. He looked up from his clothing and said, "If this is a medical visit, my normal office hours are from two till five. Unless there's some sort of emergency?" He said it with the air of a man not discounting any possibility, no matter how remote or how troublesome.

"It isn't a medical visit," Parker told him. "I want to talk to you about one of your patients, Joe Shardin."

"Oh, Joseph Shardin!" He seemed unaccountably pleased. "You knew him?"

"We were old friends. My name is Willis, Charles Willis."

"Come in, then, do come in, I'd love to chat with you." He smiled, and patted Parker's arm, and closed the door after him. "This way, come into the parlor." As he led the way into a large, airy room full of over-stuffed furniture and complicated doilies, but with no carpet on the waxed floor, he said, "Joseph Shardin was a fine man, a fine man. The kind of man you hate to lose, if you know what I mean. Sit down anywhere."

Parker was assuming that Gliffe had called to warn the doctor Parker was coming. In a town this size, everybody knowing everybody else so well, Gliffe would do that whether there was anything to cover or not. And the doctor would make believe he hadn't got any call; that he was being polite.

Settling himself in an armchair that just kept sagging downward till he was almost sitting on the floor, the doctor said, "You say you were an old friend of Joseph Shardin?"

"We were in business together," Parker told him. "Years ago." He wasn't being evasive for the hell of it; it was just he didn't know much about Joe Sheer's cover story, what Joe had been claiming around here to have retired from.

The doctor said, "He was retired now, you know."

"I know. He retired five or six years ago."

"When he moved here." The doctor nodded, as though they'd come to an important agreement about something or other, and then he said, "I believe he had relatives in Omaha; that's only thirty-five miles from here, you know. Or, no, wait a minute, he didn't have any relatives at all, did he?"

This was complicated, and for a minute Parker wasn't sure how to handle it. Joe Sheer had divided his time between a house in this town here and an apartment down in Omaha. It was in Omaha, in the safer privacy of a good-sized city, that he'd met with old friends from time to time, or occasionally took on the role of advisor to some group planning a tricky score. Here, in this little town, he'd just been a retired old man, a fisherman, a checkers player, a porch sitter, a pipe smoker. If he'd explained his trips to Omaha by letting it be known around town he had relatives down there, then by his death he'd blown that part of his cover sky-high. He didn't have any relatives in Omaha; he didn't have any relatives at all. None that would claim him, anyway.

The best way out of this was to plead ignorance: "I never knew much about his family."

"He was a solitary man," said the doctor, being a trifle portentous now, "but not a lonely one. That is, he never struck me as being lonely, the way some elderly folk are, wistful, just waiting around for the grave. It never seemed to him he'd had his fill of life, or that's the way it looked to me."

"Did you treat him long?"

"The last three years, about," said the doctor, and nodded, agreeing with himself.

"How long . . ." But the question didn't get to be

asked yet; a telephone started ringing. The doctor raised a hand for silence, and his head to listen. Looking into the middle distance, his head up and alert as a hunting dog, he listened to the phone ring, and then the murmuring silence that followed it. Parker waited with him, not saying anything.

Rubber shoes squeaked in the hallway outside, the nurse appeared in the doorway. She glanced at Parker, was affronted at his having got into the house after all, and turned her head away, saying, "It's for you, Doctor."

"Thank you. I'll take it here."

The nurse went away again, and the doctor got to his feet, saying, "Excuse me just one minute, won't you?"

"Sure."

The doctor walked over by the windows—the curtains a patterned silhouette cutting off the brightness of the day outside—and sat down on what looked like an uncomfortable antique chair next to a gleaming small table. The telephone, sitting on this table, was for some reason almost invisible; maybe because of the dark wood of the table and the pattern of the curtain behind it.

The doctor picked up the receiver and said, mildly, "Rayborn here." He listened, sitting half-turned away from Parker, the bright daylight outside the window making it difficult to make out details of his form or face. Parker had only the voice to go by.

The doctor said, "Is this who I think it is?" Then he

said, "Yes, he called." While listening this time, he
turned his head and smiled at Parker, reassuring him
he wouldn't take long, then turned back and said,
"Yes, he is." He listened, and said, "Of course not." Another space, and he said, "I'll try. I don't promise anything." A wait again, and then, "You do that.
Good-bye."

There was no reason to suppose the call had anything to do with Parker, but if it had he could supply
the other half of the conversation. If Gliffe and Rayborn and Younger were all in this together, whatever it
was, then Gliffe wouldn't just call Rayborn, he would
call both the other two. But it would take him a while
to get in touch with Younger, because Younger was
probably still standing in front of the hotel. But eventually word would get to Younger, and Younger would
check the room and see that he was gone. Then he
would call Rayborn. When Rayborn said, "Yes, he
called," that meant yes, Gliffe called. When he turned
and looked at Parker and then said, "Yes, he is," that
meant yes, Parker is here. When he said, "Of course
not," he meant of course he hadn't told Parker anything. When he said, "I'll try. I don't promise anything," he meant he'd try to keep Parker from leaving
here before Younger could show up.

If the call had anything to do with Parker at all. *If*
there was anything going on between Younger and
Rayborn and Gliffe.

Rayborn, having ended the conversation, came back
across the room. "A patient," he said, smiling, and

shrugging. "We're always on call, we general practitioners. Now, where were we?" He sat down again in the same sagging armchair.

"I was out of touch with Joe the last three years," Parker said, lying. "I wondered how long he'd had this heart trouble."

"Two years or more," the doctor said, lying right back at him. "In fact, I think it was his increasing blood pressure that first brought him to me."

Joe Sheer didn't have any history of heart trouble, right up to three months ago, Parker knew that for sure. He also knew Joe had a doctor down in Omaha. A sudden unexpected heart attack could have taken him here, and then this doctor would be in charge instead of the doctor in Omaha, but that was the only way. The story the doctor was telling was bushwah.

Which meant Captain Younger was headed this way, no question.

Parker wanted to talk to the captain, wanted to find out what the captain was trying for, but not yet. There was still more to be done first.

He got to his feet and said, "Well, I won't keep you. You must be busy."

"Not at all, not at all." The doctor struggled out of the chair, trying to look casual, saying, "I have plenty of time, office hours don't begin till two."

"I have to get back to the hotel," Parker told him, and started walking towards the front door.

The doctor trotted after him. "I haven't even offered you coffee yet. Or a drink? Surely you can spare ten minutes, I'd love to talk with you about Joe Shardin, a fine old man, there really can't be any reason for you to rush away, you just barely got here, we'll have a drink and . . ."

Parker opened the door. "Maybe I'll come back when I've got more time," he said. He looked at the doctor, who was blinking and looking winded, and still trying to be casual. "We'll have a lot to talk about," Parker told him. "Some other time." He stepped out onto the porch and let the door close behind him.

When he was a block away he looked back and saw the black Ford pulling to a stop in front of the doctor's house. But then he turned the corner and didn't see what happened next.

5

It was a smallish white clapboard house on a narrow lot in the middle of the block, flanked on both sides by houses larger than itself, but with vacant lots and fields and unfinished streeting in the block behind it. There was a driveway in from the street, running beside the house, but no garage. A gnarled apple tree stood in the middle of the back yard.

Parker had come the front way the last time, and by night. This time he was coming the back way, by day, walking across the scrubby weedy fields with his hands tucked deep in his coat pockets and his shoulder hunched against a cold breeze blowing across from his left. He came in at an angle, so he could see past the apple tree to the blank, black rear windows of the house and along the driveway to the curb out front. No face showed in the windows, and no car was parked at the curb.

In retirement, Joe had gone the whole way, even getting interested in the things retired types were supposed to be excited about, including gardening. The back yard was half lawn and half flower garden, broken up into alternative squares of each like a checkerboard, with a red slate walk meandering through it and around the apple tree and eventually to the back porch, a narrow affair with three creaking steps. A milk-company box stood on this porch, along with a broom, two empty beer cases, and a hoe. A clothes-line pulley hung from a hook on one of the porch uprights, but there was no clothes-line attached to it.

The screen door was unlocked, but the inner door wasn't. Parker tried the knob, then tried leaning on it a little, then stood and considered it a few seconds. He'd brought no tools along, nothing at all, not expecting to have to work.

There was no point fooling with it. He held the screen door open, raised his right foot, and slammed the flat of his heel into the door just above the knob. It made a hell of a racket, and the glass in the door trembled as though thinking about breaking. The second time Parker kicked it, the door gave up and opened, springing back so far and so hard it slammed into the wall. Parker stepped in, latched the screen door, and shut the door again. It wouldn't close all the way, but good enough.

He was in the kitchen, a small square room with green-checked linoleum on the floor and chintz curtains over the windows. The refrigerator was small and old and had been repainted; Parker could see the brush marks from across the room. The small wooden table and the sideboard were both clean, but in the sink were one plate, one set of silverware, one coffee cup, and two glasses. Parker opened the refrigerator and found it still working; so the electricity had never been turned off. That was stupid. The refrigerator contained some TV dinners, some hot dogs and hamburgers, a head of lettuce, an opened bottle of milk, a few twelve-ounce bottles of beer, and a quarter-pound stick of butter.

Parker shut the refrigerator door again and looked around the room. What was he looking for? He didn't know himself, exactly; just something to tell him what was going on, something to tell him how Joe had died, who had helped him if he had been helped, and what Captain Younger was up to. There might not be anything here at all, but it was the first place he should look.

He searched the rest of the kitchen and found only the stuff you'd expect to find in a bachelor's kitchen. He was all finished and ready to start on another part of the house when he remembered something. He got a table knife from the silverware drawer, took down the flour canister from its shelf, and took the top off. He poked the knife down into it, poked and pried around, and there wasn't anything in there but flour.

That wasn't right. There should have been a tobacco pouch down in there, with twenty fifty-dollar bills rolled in it; Joe Sheer's run-out money. He'd kept it there just in case he ever had to leave here too fast to close out bank accounts, and a couple of years ago he'd mentioned to Parker where he had it stashed.

Now it was gone, and it didn't make any sense for it to be gone. There was no sign anywhere around that anybody else had searched this place, which meant it wasn't taken by somebody just stumbling on it but by somebody who knew it was there all along. Who else could that be but Joe Sheer? But if Joe had taken that money, five minutes later he'd have been out of town; the thousand bucks in the flour canister was getaway financing exclusively, not to be used for anything else.

Parker put the canister back where it belonged, washed the flour from the knife, dried the knife and put it away again in the silverware drawer. Then he left the kitchen, going through a doorway that led to a central hallway about six feet long. Every room in the house led off this hallway; living room, two bedrooms, bathroom, kitchen. The cellar stairs were off this hallway, and a trap-door in the hallway ceiling led to the narrow cramped attic.

Parker went into the living room next. It was a small room, made to look even smaller because of the bulkiness and darkness of the furniture. Joe Sheer had liked an older style of furniture, the kind of heavy round stuff that went with tasselled lamp shades and fringed shawls. Parker stood just inside the doorway and looked around, and the room looked no different from the last time he'd been here. There was a new television set, but it was in an old-style cabinet that blended in well with the furniture already there.

Looking around the room, Parker happened to see the thermostat on the wall near the front door, and it occurred to him that the house was warm. He hadn't paid any attention to that when he'd first come in, because it only seemed natural that the house should be warm; but it wasn't natural at all. This house was supposed to be empty now, was supposed to have been empty for the last two or three days. Somebody should have come along by now to shut the place up.

He went over and looked at the thermostat. It was set for seventy, and the little thermometer on it read the same. So the furnace was still going, and the electricity was still turned on.

And the phone?

It was over on a rickety-looking end table next to the sofa. Parker went over and picked it up and listened for a second to the sound of the dial tone. It was still working.

He hung up the phone and looked around at the room. Somebody wanted this place to stay liveable, and he didn't know why.

He couldn't get a corner on it, not a corner.

He went on searching the place, for whatever he might find. The living room had nothing more beyond the thermostat and the telephone of interest to him. He poked and pried and found nothing. Nothing under the chairs, nothing under the sofa cushions or behind the small watercolor landscapes on the walls, nothing written or hidden in any of the few books on the shelf behind the sofa, nothing anywhere of interest.

Parker limited himself to looking in places he could get at without taking anything apart, so there still could be a million dollars in jewels hidden inside the sofa back or ten pounds of uncut heroin in the speaker cavity of the television set or several notes in invisible ink written on the lamp shades, but he doubted any of it. He finished the living room, found nothing, and went on.

Next was the bathroom, where the medicine cabinet told him Joe Sheer had been having physical trouble of all kinds in recent years, though maybe not heart disease. But, according to the junk in the medicine cabinet, he'd had piles and he'd been constipated and he'd had trouble sleeping and he'd had various troubles for which he'd been taking prescription medicines. Parker looked at the prescription bottles and they were all from the Five Corner Drug Store in Omaha, all with the name Dr. Quilley on them. According to the evidence of the medicine cabinet, Dr. Rayborn had never prescribed anything for Joe.

Before leaving the bathroom, Parker took the top off the water tank, because that was such a favorite place for people to hide things, either down in the water tank itself, wrapped in something waterproof, or taped to the inside of the top. This time there was nothing in either place.

The next room he went into was the spare bedroom, the smaller of the two. It had a bed, a dresser, a throw rug, and a kitchen chair in it, because Joe did, every once in a great while, have company that stayed over, somebody like Parker. He preferred most of the time to meet with his friends from his old life down in the apartment in Omaha, but every once in a while—particularly when the weather was good—he brought a house guest out to see him living the good life in the little town of Sagamore.

Now, the bed was made, the dresser was empty, and the closet was emptier. There was nothing in this room at all, no messages for Parker about anything. Except maybe that Joe hadn't had any company that stayed over for some time.

Joe's own bedroom was a different proposition. It wasn't as neat as the rest of the house. From the looks of it, it could have been searched two or three times already, and every time by impatient slobs. But Parker knew this was normal, the way Joe had always kept his bedroom. The rest of the house could be neat and clean, and usually was, but his bedroom had to be a mess. Maybe it was because he'd taken one fall, back when he was young, and had spent four years sleeping in the barren metallic neatness of a jail cell.

It took a long time to go through Joe's bedroom, and when he was done Parker had learned nothing. Throughout the whole house, nothing he knew of was missing except the thousand bucks from the flour canister. The telephone and utilities were still on, there was additional proof that Dr. Rayborn had been lying, and there was no sign at all that anyone else had made a search through here. He knew a few facts and no reasons.

There were still two places to look, the attic and the cellar. He stood in the central hall and considered, looking up at the trap-door in the ceiling but finally deciding to let the attic wait till last. He turned and opened the cellar door, and something with a sack over its head came lunging up out of the darkness, swinging something that whistled like the wind as it came around and smashed into the side of Parker's head. Parker had time to feel his hand scrape along burlap, time to see the cellar stairs rushing in on a long curve towards him, getting bigger and bigger, and then he went out like a burned-out bulb.

6

The voice was a centipede, a long twisty bug with needle-sharp feet running back and forth on the left side of his face, driving its needle feet into the bone beside his eye and into his cheekbone and into the bone above his ear. His face hurt like fury; it hurt every time the voice sounded, and the voice sounded all the time. He thrashed a little in impotent rage, wanting the voice to stop hurting the side of his face.

Moving like that brought him up out of it a bit more, far enough out so he could begin to separate sensations, differentiate between hearing the voice in his ears and feeling the pains on the side of his face, begin to know they weren't connected, not two parts of the same thing after all but just two separate sensations that had both helped to drag him back to consciousness.

From there, it was practically no step at all to come up far enough to begin to wonder what the voice was saying, and almost immediately to begin to separate the words and discover what they meant:

". . . out of it. Come on, Willis, snap out of it. I don't have all day. Get with it, fella, get with it."

Now there was something else added to it all; somebody poking and pushing at his left shoulder. He complained, and moved around again, twisting on the concrete floor, and all at once he was out of it completely, eyes open, brain working. He sat up and stared into the face of Captain Younger.

They were in a basement, garishly lit by bare bulbs in fixtures along the cental beam. The concrete floor was painted a greyish blue. Captain Younger was sitting on the next-to-the-bottom step of the stairs leading up to the main floor, and Parker had been lying on his back right in front of the stairs.

Captain Younger said, "You conscious now?"

Parker said, "I was slugged."

"You sure you didn't fall downstairs?"

Parker shrugged. He was still woozy, having trouble thinking, having trouble making things connect so they made sense. The best thing for now was to say not much of anything; otherwise he might say something stupid and make trouble for himself.

Captain Younger pointed and said, "You chopped up the side of your face there pretty good."

Parker said nothing. He closed his eyes and tried to make his brain come into focus.

Captain Younger said, "Don't pass out again. I got questions for you."

"Don't worry."

"Like for instance," Captain Younger said, "what were you digging for?"

Parker opened his eyes. "What?"

Captain Younger pointed off to the right. "What were you digging for, Willis? What were you trying to find?"

Parker turned his head, slowly, and looked over where the captain was pointing. There was a coal-bin over there, with wooden slat sides. There wasn't any coal in the coal-bin, because the furnace had long since been converted to oil, and the concrete floor didn't extend into the coal-bin. The coal-bin had a dirt floor, most of which had been dug into. A big mound of dirt was out on the concrete.

Captain Younger said, "Well?"

"I didn't do that."

"Come on, Willis, you think I'm stupid?"

Parker squinted up at him, trying to think. Younger wasn't kidding around; he really did think Parker had done that digging. So Parker's first thought, that Younger or somebody working for Younger had been down in the cellar and had slugged him, was probably wrong. There was somebody else in this, too, somebody Younger didn't know anything about.

Tiftus? Could it possibly be Tiftus? Could that little bastard have been the one down here?

Captain Younger leaned forward, his round face inches from Parker's. A thin sheen of perspiration covered his face, glinting like wet varnish. In a hoarser and quieter tone, he said, "I know what you're looking for, Willis. I knew what you were up to the second you came to town. You found out the old bastard was dead and you figured to just come in here and have everything your own way."

He wasn't making any sense at all. Parker shook his head and said, "You're talking Chinese. I'm going to stand up now."

"Go right ahead."

Parker reached out and grabbed the staircase banister and used it to drag himself up to standing. Captain Younger had got to his feet in the meantime and retreated up three more steps, so he was out of Parker's reach.

Parker looked up at him and said, "Let's go upstairs."

"What were you digging for, Willis?"

"It's the way I exercise." He put his hand on the banister again, and started up the steps.

Captain Younger retreated backwards up the stairs, looking affronted. "You'll tell me, Willis," he said. His voice was a little shrill. "You'll tell me anything I want to know. Before I'm done with you . . ." He didn't finish the sentence; he'd reached the top of the stairs. He backed out of the way and glared, and Parker came on up the stairs and through the hall and into the bathroom.

The face he looked at in the mirror over the sink was a mess. The left side of it, from the jawline up into the hair above his ear, was all mottled red and purple and black, as though somebody had thrown bright-colored mud on him. A puffiness and darkness was developing around his left eye; unless he did something about it soon, he was going to have a hell of a shiner.

Captain Younger came and stood in the doorway and said, "That's a real job you did on yourself."

"Call your tame doctor, I need him."

"Sure, Willis. Just as soon as you tell me what I want to know."

Parker was feeling impatient, and he was still rocky from having been slugged, so he said more than he would have usually. He turned to look at Captain Younger and say, "You know everything already. You know I was digging down there without a shovel, and you know I hit myself on the side of the face. You know what I was looking for. What else do you want?"

"What was that you said? About the shovel?" Captain Younger was so startled he almost crossed the threshold and got close enough for Parker to reach out for him.

Parker said, "Did you see a shovel down there? What do you think the guy hit me with?"

All of a sudden there was a gun in Captain Younger's hand. "So you found it," he said. "You had an accomplice, and you found it, and he took off with it."

"With what? When do you start making sense?"

"Where's he going, Willis? There's still a chance for you to get a cut. You tell me where he's going, what he looks like, what name he travels under. I can get out an alarm on him, have him picked up for questioning no matter where he goes. You can't get him, but I can."

Parker shook his head. "There's a hell of a lot of morons with guns," he said. "I talk to you after I see the doctor."

Captain Younger seemed to consider for a minute, and then he said, "So you're not worried about wasting time. So maybe you *know* where he's going."

Parker waited. Sooner or later Younger was going to have to start making sense.

Younger motioned with the gun. "All right, Willis," he said. "Let's go into the living room. I'll call Dr. Rayborn for you. He can come right over here and take care of you, and then we'll talk. I'm not taking you down to headquarters; I'm keeping you right here, and when we're done with the doctor you'll tell me everything I want to know."

They walked into the living room, Parker first, and Parker settled himself in an overstuffed armchair where the light from the windows was all behind him, where Captain Younger wouldn't be able to see his face very well. Younger got on the phone and made his call and then sat down fat and smug on the sofa, the gun held casually in his lap. His brown suit was baggy and creaseless, his cowboy hat was tipped back on his head. He looked like a yokel Khrushchev.

They sat in silence a minute or two, and then Younger said, "I know what you think. You think I'm just another hick cop. Well, that's all right, Willis, I don't mind. You go on thinking that, you think that just as long as you can. Dr. Rayborn'll be here in a little while, and he'll get you all fixed up nice and new, and then you can start telling me all about yourself and what your connection was with Joe Sheer."

It took Parker a few seconds to realize that Captain Younger had just said Joe's real name, not the cover name he'd been buried under. Parker squinted, and saw Captain Younger sitting over there pleased and contented, smiling like the Cheshire cat.

1

. . . All about yourself and what your connection was with Joe Sheer."

That was easy. What his connection was with Joe Sheer most recently, he had come up to this rotten little town to find out if it was going to be necessary to kill Joe Sheer or not. And all about himself, that was even easier; he was a thief.

Once or twice a year, Parker was in on an institutional robbery—the robbing from organizations rather than from individuals. It wasn't out of humanity that he limited himself to organizations, it was just that organizations had more money than individuals; organizations like banks or jewelry stores or one of those firms that still paid its employees in cash.

Parker wasn't a single-o. He always worked with a pickup group gathered for that single specific job. Every man was a specialist, and Parker's specialties were two: planning and violence. Other men were specialists in opening safes or scaling walls or making up blueprints from nothing more than observation, but Parker was a specialist at planning an operation so it ran smoothly, and at stopping any outsider who might be thinking of lousing things up.

It was rare for a job to take more than a month in the planning and the operation, so it was rare for Parker to spend more than a month to six weeks a year at his work. The rest of the time he lived on the proceeds, usually in a coastal resort center, under the name Charles Willis. Willis owned pieces of small businesses—parking lots and laundromats and things like that—here and there around the country; they never brought him a dime, but they justified his income on his Federal tax forms. As Charles Willis he had a complete background, documents and everything, enough to satisfy anybody.

He had been Charles Willis in Miami Beach, spending the money from his last job—at a place called Copper Canyon, North Dakota, in the course of which he'd met the woman he was living with now—when the first letter had come from Joe Sheer. It had read:

Parker,

I think I got some trouble here, but I'll take care of it. But maybe you better not try to get in touch with me for a while, until I get everything squared away again. I'm not down in my place in Omaha, but staying up here in my house in Sagamore. If anybody tries to get in touch with you through me for the next while I'll have to tell them to go to you direct if I'm sure of who it is. If I'm not sure, I'll just play dumb, until this trouble straightens itself out. I'll let you know when everything is okay again.

Joe

Joe Sheer was an old-time jugger who'd cracked his first safe the other side of the First World War. He wasn't working anymore now, but in his day he'd been one of the best safe and vault men in the business. There wasn't a bank vault made he couldn't open, and he worked at staying on top of the profession. Under three or four names, at different addresses around the country, he got all the trade papers and promotional copy from every safe and vault manufacturer, private protective association, and manufacturer of locks and burglar alarms; and he got all the banking association trade journals. Nor was he, like most juggers, limited in his methods; he could use nitro or the torch or the hammer or a drill, whatever was best for the particular job. When he was active, he'd been in steady demand.

But about five years ago he'd retired. Like Parker, like most of the professionals in this business, he'd had a cover name for years, complete with a faked-up way of earning a livelihood and all the documents you could ask for to prove identity. Among those documents was a Social Security card. When, shortly after his sixty-fifth birthday, he began to receive Social Security payments, Joe Sheer laughed for a week and then retired. His Social Security payments didn't cover the standard of living he was used to, but they didn't have to; he'd salted away some of his take over the years, enough to keep him going clear to the other side of the actuarial tables.

Joe had retired from the active side of the business, but not from the profession entirely. He still sat in on occasional planning sessions for a small piece of the action, and he operated as an answering service of sorts for Parker and a few other guys in the business.

The thing was, when Parker was being Charles Willis, he didn't want anybody contacting him as Parker. Almost everybody else in the business felt the same way; they didn't want other people in the business busting in on them when they were using their cover identities. So Parker, like a lot of others, had a friend who relayed any messages that might come along, who served as the one link between Parker and Charles Willis. Joe Sheer was the friend. If anyone in the business wanted to get in touch with Parker, he had to contact Joe Sheer, tell Joe the story, and wait for Joe to pass the word on to Parker. If Parker then felt like it, he would meet the other guy wherever the original message had said. If he didn't feel like it, there was no answer. His not showing up was its own answer.

For the last five years, that had been the main connection between Parker and Joe Sheer, the message bit. Plus, one time a couple years ago, he'd holed up at Joe's place in Omaha while Joe got him set up for a plastic surgeon to give him a new face; the one he'd carried around till then had got unpopular. Since then, except for occasional messages from other people through Joe, Parker had had no direct contact with him.

When he got the letter, he wondered a little what sort of trouble Joe was in, but since Joe had sounded confident that he could take care of it himself, and since in their business worrying about one's own self was a full-time job, Parker hadn't wasted any sleep over Joe Sheer. He was still flush from the Copper Canyon job anyway, and not looking for work, so it didn't matter to him if the messenger service broke down for a while.

The second letter came a month later. It read:

Parker,

You got to excuse an old man. I need help. You know I never in my life pushed for anybody to get me out of any trouble, but I'm getting old and rusty and scared. If you want to tell me to go to hell that's okay, but if you got the time and inclination I could use a hand up here. I don't promise you any profit out of it at all. In fact I don't see how you could break even on travel expenses unless I pay for them, and I will. If you got a woman, bring her along and I'll pay for her too. A young hardcase like you could take care of this problem of mine with no sweat, and sit around and drink beer a while afterwards. This isn't trouble I would have thought twice about ten years ago, but now is another story. Anyway, if you're coming, just come, and if you're not then don't and I won't hold it against you. Whatever you do for God sake don't call me on the telephone.

Joe

Parker read the letter three times before he made up his mind about it. It sounded like Joe Sheer's way of speaking and writing, but it sure as hell didn't sound like anything Joe Sheer would ever say. There were things men in their business might do for each other, like hide each other out if the heat wasn't too strong or stake each other if there were funds to spare, but they just wouldn't write this kind of letter to one another. A man didn't ask for help in a personal problem in the first place. In the second place, if a man asked for help about anything at all, he never said a word about *paying* for the help; he might say something about how big a piece of the action the helper might expect, but that was something else again. This business of offering to pay transportation was just cheap.

In the third place, a man never apologized for what cards he'd been dealt; what did Joe Sheer think all of a sudden at age seventy, he was the captain of his fate? A man was what the world decided he would be, and where the world decided he would be, and in the condition the world had chosen for him. If the world had decided to deal Joe a bad hand this time, it wasn't up to him to apologize for not having better cards.

But that was something Joe already knew, or had known. Now, from the looks of this letter, he'd forgotten it.

When he finally made up his mind it was really Joe Sheer who had written that letter, Parker pulled out a suitcase and started packing. It wasn't for Joe Sheer that he packed, or that he called the airport and made a reservation on the next plane for Omaha. As far as he was concerned, Joe could drop dead right now and that would be fine with Parker. In fact that would be better; it would save him a trip.

He was going for himself. He was going because in Joe's letter he saw a danger to himself much more obvious and lethal than any danger Joe had been trying to describe. What he saw was the shaky penmanship and shaky mentality of an old man. Joe was going senile. At seventy, he'd lost every trace of the code of ethics he'd lived by all his adult life.

But he hadn't lost Parker's name and address.

Joe Sheer could crucify Parker, he could nail him to the wall with a hundred nails. He knew him by his old face, because who else but Joe Sheer had set Parker up with the plastic surgeon? He knew Parker's cover name, he knew twenty or twenty-five jobs Parker had been connected with, he knew enough about Parker to skin him alive.

Up till now that hadn't meant anything, because Joe had also known what sort of world he lived in and what his role was in that world. But not anymore. Joe Sheer was just an old jugger now, turned shaky and rusty—he'd said it himself—shaky and rusty and scared, an old jugger ready to trade every man he'd ever worked with for a nice soft mattress and a nice warm radiator and a little peace of mind.

So Parker packed a suitcase and took a cab from the hotel and a plane from the airport and flew north and west across the country to see what it would take to protect himself from Joe Sheer.

He arrived at Omaha on Tuesday afternoon, switched from plane to train, got to the town of Sagamore Tuesday evening, and registered at the Sagamore Hotel. He didn't plan on staying at Joe's place this time because he didn't know what his relationship was going to be with Joe this time. And he used the Charles Willis name because that was the name he always used with Joe. He didn't know then that this was going to get complicated, that a local cop would be in the act before noon the next day; if he'd known it, he would have used some other name.

No tourist had ever stayed at the Sagamore Hotel; traveling men only. Sagamore was not a tourist attraction, nor was it near any tourist attraction, nor on any possible route to any tourist attraction. A few smallish but dirty factories supported the town, and traveling men supported the Sagamore Hotel. The desk clerk looked at Parker and couldn't figure out for the life of him who or what Parker was. He spent the rest of the night thinking about it and finally decided that if Parker sold anything it was either liquor or guns.

Later that night, Parker went over to Joe's house to have a talk with him and see how the land lay. He walked, both because it was a small town where nothing was impossibly far from anything else and because in the future he might not want anybody able to state with certainty that Charles Willis had been in that neighborhood tonight.

When he got to the house it was all in darkness, though it was only a little after eight. He stood on the porch and rang the doorbell, telling himself that senile old men sometimes sat in the dark and sometimes took evening naps, and then a teenage kid called him from the porch of the house next door and told him Mr. Shardin had died yesterday, yes, the funeral was to be tomorrow morning, yes, it was all very sudden.

Too sudden.

Parker went back to the hotel room to think it out. By the time he'd received that second letter from Joe, the old man had already been dead. What had happened to him? What sort of trouble had he been talking about? Was it anything that could eventually get back to Parker? He remembered, in that first letter, Joe had made a point of saying he'd have to cut out the messenger service until after he got everything straightened out.

Joe was dead, but that didn't solve everything after all. Parker still had to know how Joe had died, and who had been causing what kind of trouble, and if there was now anyone in the town of Sagamore who could later on cause trouble for Parker or Charles Willis. He had to know now, and not wait for it to come looking for him, because then it would be too late.

So he stayed over that night, and in the morning he went down and asked the desk clerk about the local paper, but the local paper was a weekly that came out on Thursday, so what Parker wanted was the district paper, and the district paper office was over in Lyn-brooke, seven miles away.

Across the street from the hotel was the railroad sta-tion, and in front of it was parked a taxi, a dusty black Chevrolet four or five years old. Parker hired it to take him to Lynbrooke and back. He rode out there and picked up yesterday's paper. When he came out of the newspaper office there was a black Ford parked be-hind the Chevy, and a stocky man in brown business suit and tan cowboy hat was leaning against the side of the Chevy, talking in a lazy way with the driver sitting behind the wheel. He went away when Parker came along, and Parker saw him get into the black Ford.

Riding back to Sagamore, the black Ford stayed on their tail. After a couple of miles, Parker said to the driver, "Who's the guy in the cowboy hat?"

"Him? The guy talking to me?" The driver was in his late twenties, wearing an Army Ike jacket and too-long dry blond hair. A dark inverted V on the sleeve of the jacket showed where he'd stripped off the insignia of the highest rank he'd ever held: Pfc. He had a sharp narrow face, with the bone structure clear and plain around the hollows of the eyes. When he spoke, old frustrations trembled behind his voice.

Parker said, "He smelled like law. Is he?"

"You could say that."

"What kind of law?"

"The rotten kind."

"I mean what level. State, local, county, what is he?"

"Town. He runs the town police force, in Sagamore."

Parker flicked his cigarette out of the window. "How big's the town police force?"

The driver shrugged. "Maybe twelve, fifteen men, I don't know."

"Big responsibility. What do they call him, commissioner?"

"Captain. He's got a couple lieutenants and everybody else is sergeants."

Parker frowned. The driver was willing enough to talk but he didn't know how. It was like pulling teeth, getting anything from him. He said, "This captain, he got a name?"

"Younger, Captain Younger."

"What did he want to know about me?"

"Who said he wanted to know about you? We were just talking."

"Sure." Parker shrugged, and looked back. The Ford was indolently behind them. He said, "How come you aren't one of his sergeants?"

The driver didn't say anything for a minute. He hunched over the wheel more than he had, and the Chevy picked up speed. But after a few seconds the speed slackened off again, and the driver said, so low that Parker could barely hear it, "I got a job."

"Sure."

After that they rode in silence, back to Sagamore and the hotel. Then, as Parker was paying him, the driver said quickly, "He wanted to know did I know your name, did you say anything on the way out, had I ever seen you around town before anywhere, did you say what you wanted from the district paper, did you mention any names at all."

"Thanks."

"Even if I'd known anything, I wouldn't have told that bastard."

Parker got out of the car and stood a second while the driver took the Chevy around a sweeping U-turn and put it in its parking slot across the street in front of the railroad station.

The Ford pulled to the curb a few yards to Parker's left. Captain Younger climbed heavily out of it, pulled a handkerchief from his hip pocket, took off his cowboy hat, wiped his forehead and the sweatband with the handkerchief, and put hat and handkerchief back where he'd got them. Out of his inside coat pocket he pulled a cigar and made a long ceremony out of unwrapping it and getting it ready to smoke. He didn't look at Parker at all.

Parker turned and went on into the hotel. It was a small building, only four stories high, but spread out in a rambling manner, and with a lobby far too broad and long for the rest of the place. Green leather sofas were scattered here and there over the dark orange carpeting in the lobby, and at the far end one lone man stood like a joke behind the broad sweep of desk.

Parker went upstairs, and Captain Younger stayed on plant out in front of the hotel.

Then, everywhere else Parker went, it kept coming back to Captain Younger, and it wound up in Joe

Sheer's house, the two of them face to face, Parker and Captain Younger, and Parker still didn't know a damn thing.

Except he had trouble.

PART TWO

1

Dr. Rayborn was a poor liar, but a good doctor. He didn't ask any questions, either of Captain Younger or Parker, but went right to work on Parker's face. He cleaned the bruises with cotton, and put a stinging ointment on a couple of the worst places, and then sprayed something on the side of his face out of a pressurized can. The spray was freezing cold at first, but it cut through the pain and gradually numbed the side of Parker's face like Novocain.

All through it, nobody talked. Younger watched Parker and Parker watched the doctor, and the doctor watched his own hands. He wouldn't meet anybody's eye. Through his efficiency, nervousness glittered, like the sky seen through an intermittent overcast.

When at last he was finished and putting his tools back in his black bag, Younger said to him, "This is just between us fellas, Larry."

Not looking up from his bag, the doctor said, "This

is the end, Abner, the last straw. No more. Don't call me again."

"*I* didn't do that to him," Younger said. "He fell downstairs. Isn't that right, Willis?"

Parker didn't say anything.

Dr. Rayborn said, "He didn't get that from falling downstairs. Don't lie to me, Abner, I'm not a fool."

"Well, I say *I* didn't do it. God damn it, Willis, did I lay a hand on you?"

Still Parker didn't say anything. Face expressionless, he watched the two of them. Sooner or later he'd want another private talk with Dr. Rayborn, the weak link.

The doctor was saying, "I don't care about the details, Abner. I don't want to know about them. I didn't want to know about—"

"Shut your mouth!"

The doctor was suddenly twice as nervous. He shut his bag with a loud click, and his eyes kept darting over to look at Parker. Parker watched him with flat expressionless eyes.

Younger said, "You're gonna get yourself in trouble." He pointed a finger at the doctor and jabbed the finger in the air. "You're gonna get *everybody* in trouble. Now, you just watch yourself."

"I'm sorry. I—"

"You just won't quit talking, will you? Go on home, Larry, I'll call you later on."

"All right." He picked up his bag and stood there looking nervous and agitated. "Abner," he said, "I don't want any more. This is the last time."

"I'll call you later."

"I mean it, Abner."

"I said I'll call you later."

Rayborn still hesitated a few seconds longer and then finally gave a weak man's shrug and turned away and went on out the front door. He closed it behind himself, and in the silence that followed, Younger puffed out a blue Disney cloud of cigar smoke and said, "That man is a weak sister. Nothing but a weak sister."

Parker swiveled his eyes without moving his head. He watched Younger, and waited to see what would happen next. His face felt strange, the left side dead and numb.

Captain Younger sighed massively and got to his feet. The cigar was in his left hand, the gun in his right. His cowboy hat was tipped back on his head, his shirt collar was open and tie loosened, his suit jacket was unbuttoned, and his trousers were hooked under his paunch. He looked like a man with nothing but time and patience. He was a lot more sure of himself now, after the session with Rayborn, and he was showing it.

He walked around the room a little bit, still keeping well away from Parker, and finally he said, "The question is, do you know where it is or don't you? That's the question."

Parker waited; nothing to say yet, nothing to respond to.

"At first, I figured you did know, and all I had to do

was keep you in sight, you'd lead me straight to it. But now I don't think so. It isn't here. I don't believe for a minute it's in this house, so you poking around here means you don't know any more than anybody. Is that right?"

Parker couldn't tell yet whether it would be best to claim to know nothing or everything, so he went on waiting.

Younger had been trying some rudimentary kind of psychology, because now he said, "Or *is* it here? Do you know for *sure* it's here? How come you were digging in the cellar?"

Parker shook his head, but didn't say anything.

"All right, not you, your partner. The little bastard in the funny clothes. You were seen punching him in the face right out on the sidewalk this afternoon, what do you think of that?"

"Not much."

"He's your partner, isn't he?"

"No."

"He was digging down there, wasn't he?"

"Maybe it was him, maybe not. The guy that hit me had a burlap bag over his head."

"Oh, stop that! You went down there *with* him! What do you think I am?"

Parker said, "I think you're a hick and a moron and a bigmouth and yellow from your head to your ass."

The captain stopped in his tracks and stared at Parker. His face got red, and his hand on the gun got white. He opened his mouth three times before he managed to say anything, and then the words came out in a strangled whisper:

"I could kill you, Willis, don't you know that? I run this town, I run it, I run the police force. I could kill you, right here and now, shoot you down dead at my feet, and nobody'd ever say a word to me about it. You're surely wanted somewhere for something, an old friend of Joe Sheer's like you, you've got to be on somebody's wanted list. I caught you burglarizing the house and when I tried to arrest you, you jumped me and I shot you in self-defense. Don't you know that? I could kill you right now and not think twice about it."

"If you kill me," Parker told him, "you'll never know anything."

"I won't? I won't?" For some reason, that seemed to make Younger even madder than before. "Explain that," he said. "Make it snappy, you, explain yourself. By God, I *will* kill you! You give me a reason not to do it, just one good reason not to shoot you down this minute."

Parker said, "I went to see Gliffe."

Younger waited, but Parker didn't say any more. Finally, Younger said, "So what? What's that supposed to mean?"

"You figure it out."

"What the hell are you talking about?"

"You don't understand what's going on, Younger. You got a theory and it doesn't work, it's full of holes. There's some little man I'm supposed to be partners with, but I'm seen hitting him on the street and he hits me with a shovel down in the cellar here. You call that partners? Does your theory tell you why I went to see Gliffe and Rayborn? Does it tell you why I went to Lynbrooke?"

"To get the paper, what are you talking about? I know what you went to Lynbrooke for, to get the paper."

"Why? Why did I want the paper?"

Younger was looking more and more baffled, more and more irritated, more and more impatient and enraged. He waved his arms wildly, shouting, "What the hell do I care? I don't care what you wanted the goddam paper for, what do I care about that? I know what you came to this town for, don't give me a lot of—"

The shrilling of the telephone cut into his hollering and stopped it like turning off a radio. In the silence after the first ring they looked at one another, Younger's eyes wide as though some sort of superstition had him in its grip, Parker watching and waiting.

The phone shrilled a second time. Younger shook his head and in the silence this time said, "It's your partner, calling you. But *I'll* answer the phone, Willis, what do you think of that?"

There was nothing to say. Younger was a moron with a title, that's all; give a moron authority and after a while he forgets he's a moron.

Younger went over and picked up the phone before it could make its noise a third time. He held it carefully to his face, as though still a little afraid it might explode. Cautiously he said, "Hello? Hello?"

As Parker watched, an expression of relief washed over Younger's face and he said, "Yes, this is he, this is he." He hunched over the phone, listening as though for a state secret; then he frowned and half turned to peer at Parker, and said, "Who? Local?" He kept watching Parker as he listened to the answer, and then he turned away again and said, his voice lower than before, "How long?"

Parker knew something was wrong, but not how bad or if it connected with him. He watched and waited and wondered if in a minute or two he was going to have to jump Younger and kill him and start covering his tracks around here.

This thing was just getting worse and worse, and now he was in it too deep to get out again, and the worst part was he was in it using the Charles Willis name, the safe name, the cover name, the background name. If the Charles Willis name got loused up he'd have to start all over again from scratch.

He looked at his hands. The tips of those fingers were on file in Washington, listed under the name Ronald Casper. Ronald Casper was wanted for killing a prison-farm guard in California, the result of a bad time he'd had with his now-dead wife a few years ago. Parker himself was probably wanted for a few robberies here and there, though without the connecting link of fingerprints. But up till now Charles Willis wasn't wanted anywhere.

He couldn't afford to have Younger book him, not for anything, not even for spitting on the sidewalk. He couldn't afford to have Charles Willis connected up with Ronald Casper, the two names meeting in the middle at Parker. Somehow he had to come out of this with the Willis name still safe.

If he'd known Joe was dead, known there would be this trouble, he wouldn't have used the Willis name in the first place. If he'd known what it was going to be like, he wouldn't have come in here at all.

Waiting for Younger, waiting to find out how much new trouble this phone call meant, he tried to work out how to keep the Willis name safe if worse came to worst. He'd have to get rid of Younger, and Gliffe and Rayborn too, cover himself somehow with the hotel reservations, get back to Miami double-quick, and work up some sort of alibi placing him there the whole time. It would be complicated, and it would all have to be done fast. But he believed it could be done; the necessary can always be done.

Over there on the phone, Younger was saying, "I'll be right there. And leave the state boys out of this one, we'll do it ourselves."

Parker lit a cigarette and shifted forward on the sofa so he could get to his feet faster if he had to.

Younger hung up the phone and turned to look at Parker. He was frowning again, looking baffled. "All right," he said. "Maybe you're right."

"Right about what?"

"Things I don't know, things I got to find out."

Parker watched him, wondering what had happened to change Younger this way.

Younger said, "They just found your partner clubbed to death, it looks like with a shovel." He nodded. "In your hotel room," he said.

"*My* room?"

"That's what I say." Younger looked down at the gun in his hand as though he'd never seen it before. He shook his head and tucked the gun away inside his coat. "Come on. Let's go see him."

2

The room was full of law. Apparently somebody on Younger's force had invited the state police to attend after all; the pack of technical men, with their cameras and chalk, powders and notebooks and little white envelopes, all seemed too professional, too sleek, too quiet and efficient to be any part of the local law.

The local law was three dough-faced farm hands in rumpled blue uniforms, standing around the room looking for traffic to direct.

Parker stood there near the door and watched. When they'd come in, Younger had looked at the pros at work, had cursed under his breath, and had told Parker, "You wait right there. Don't talk to nobody." Now he was across the room talking to the guy who must be in charge of the state men: a tall, straight, strong-looking guy with a grey crewcut and a professor's face.

Parker watched and waited. From where he was standing, he could see Tiftus on the floor next to the bed. He wasn't much to look at. He'd been turned away, so the shovel—or whatever the guy had used—had hit him on the back of the head, cracking his skull like so many pieces of egg shell. He'd fallen on his face, blood and hair had mixed together to make a little thatched roof on the back of his head, and he'd died.

The technicians worked around him now as though they expected to launch him into space.

Across the room, Younger wasn't being happy. He was trying to argue, but he wasn't winning. The state man was being polite but firm, and Parker could see that Younger didn't stand a chance.

Younger saw it too, after a while, and gave up. He came back over to Parker and said, "We got to talk."

"We do?"

"Out in the hall."

Parker knew it was a dumb move, but this was Younger's party right now. He followed Younger out to the hall, feeling the state man's eyes on his back all the way.

In the hall, down a way from the door, Younger turned and, standing close to the wall, said, "You're in the clear on killing him."

"And?"

"With me," Younger said. "*I* know you're in the clear. They don't."

"Why not?"

Younger was taking some satisfaction from this exchange, evening the score for losing with the state man. He took his time. "They know when he was killed. Within half an hour they know it. I was already with you then. I'm your alibi."

Parker said, "And I'm yours."

Younger was surprised. "Mine? What the hell do I need with an alibi?"

"You're looking for something, and so was Tiftus."

"And so are you, God damn it."

Parker shrugged.

Younger said, "We don't have much time, Willis, don't waste it with a lot of crap. I'm your alibi, that's the point, I'm your alibi if I want to be. If I don't want to be, you've had it."

"You didn't say anything yet?"

"Not a word. Regan, the guy I was talking to, he wants to ask you some questions."

"Why?"

"Because it's your room. Because you're a stranger here and so is that guy whatchamacallim, and because you knew each other."

Parker nodded. "So you want to deal."

"Partners," Younger told him. "Fifty-fifty split, all the way."

"I don't know where the stuff is."

"So we'll both look for it, we'll team up." Younger jabbed a thumb at the room they'd just left. "*Somebody* killed him," he said. "It wasn't you and it wasn't me. So there's somebody else in this. We got to stick together for our own good."

The best thing now was to ride along with Younger

and look for a chance to get the edge. Parker said, "It's a deal."

Younger seemed relieved. "That's good," he said. "We still got to let Regan talk to you, but don't worry, I'll be right there with you."

Parker wasn't worried. He said, "Afterwards, I want to get out of the hotel."

Younger was suddenly suspicious. "Why? Where you want to go?"

"Back to Joe's house."

"We look *together*, Willis."

"Not to look, to live. To stay."

"Why?"

"There's no cops there."

Younger said, "You don't figure to skip, do you?"

"And leave it all for you?"

It was the right thing to say. Younger nodded and said, "All right, then. We'll go back together. I'll tell you one thing, I don't think it's in the house. I been through that house, and I don't think it's there. I didn't dig in the cellar, but I looked around there and I didn't see any sign *he'd* been digging, and I would have. He hid it good, the old bastard." Younger shook his head, and then smiled. "But we'll find it, won't we?"

"Sure."

It made Younger happy to think so. "Come on," he said. "Let's go talk to Regan."

3

Sitting in front of the desk, Parker smoked a cigarette and waited for Regan to come back. Behind him, Younger paced back and forth, back and forth, puffing on a cigar and muttering to himself.

They were in the hotel manager's office; Regan had commandeered it for his interviews. He had phoned the manager from Parker's room and then had escorted Parker and Younger down in the elevator. It was clear he didn't have any use for Younger; he treated Younger with the curt, polite contempt of a professional forced to deal with an incompetent in the same profession. It was also clear he didn't yet know what to make of Parker, and was waiting to learn more.

Once in the manager's office, Regan remembered something else he had to do, excused himself, and left Younger and Parker alone. Parker said to Younger, "Could this place be bugged?"

"What? Of course not."

Parker shook his head. He couldn't figure out what

Regan was up to. He had to know Parker and Younger had already talked together in the hall, and he had to know they'd arrived at the room together in the first place. So what was Regan up to?

Given his choice, Parker would have sided with Regan against Younger rather than the other way around. Given his choice, Parker would have picked almost anyone for a partner instead of Younger; even Tiftus. But he didn't have a choice, so he had to do the best he could with what he had.

He said, "Don't talk too much when he's asking me questions. Let me answer myself."

"You don't have to worry about me," Younger said. He was offended.

"Yes I do. You don't talk unless Regan asks you a direct question, and then all you do is answer it."

"I'll take care of myself, Willis. You just take care of you." Younger was really hot under the collar. He stalked back and forth and blew cigar smoke everywhere.

Parker stopped. He didn't want Younger lousing things up for spite, and he was just dumb enough to do it if he was pushed hard enough.

Regan came back in, finally, and said, "Sorry to keep you waiting, Mr. Willis. Willis, isn't it?"

"Yes, Willis. Charles Willis."

"Of course. Abner, sit down, why don't you?" Regan went around behind the manager's desk and sat down there like a man about to get caught up on his work.

"Could I see some identification, Mr. Willis? Just for the record."

Parker got out his wallet and put it, open, on the desk. "Everything in there," he said. "Go on through it."

"Ah, thank you, that won't be necessary." Regan smiled briefly and politely at the wallet, and said to Younger, "I'm having one of my stenographers in, so you won't have to call yours. I'll send you a copy, of course."

Parker looked at Younger, and saw that Younger hadn't thought about a stenographer at all, that Regan had just gone out of his way to insult Younger, and that Younger had caught the insult in the midsection. But Younger didn't say anything, not a word.

Regan turned to Parker and said, "As I understand it, you and Mr. Tiftus were in business together."

Parker shook his head. "Not me. You've got that wrong."

"I do?" Regan reached out and patted Parker's wallet, offhandedly, the way another man might doodle. "That was my understanding," he said. "You knew Mr. Tiftus in some other way, then?"

"I'd met him before."

"Yes, of course."

"In Miami, at the dog track. He owned a few dogs."

"Ah, he was in racing. And are you in racing, Mr. Willis?"

"No, I'm in business."

"Business? May I ask what business?"

"Various businesses. Real estate, parking lots, laundromats, here and there across the country." Parker pointed at the wallet. "There's papers on some of it in there."

But Regan wouldn't give any attention to the wallet. He said, "Then you and Mr. Tiftus didn't come here together."

"No."

"It was just coincidence you happened to meet here again."

Parker shook his head. "No, it wasn't."

Regan seemed surprised. "It wasn't coincidence? You mean you'd planned to meet here?"

"No. I didn't know I'd see him here at all. But I came here for Joe Shardin's funeral, and I guess Tiftus did, too. You meet somebody at the funeral of a guy you both knew, that isn't coincidence."

Regan turned his head and looked at Younger. "Shardin?"

"Retired man," Younger told him. "Just died a few days ago, buried this morning."

"Native?"

"Lived here about five years."

Regan gave his attention back to Parker. "So you both came here for this man Shardin's funeral."

"I couldn't say. I know I did, and I figure he did, but I don't know about him for sure."

"And about his slaying? Do you have any ideas about that?"

Parker shook his head.

Regan nodded, smiled, and said, "Well, we won't take much longer. I appreciate your co-operation, Mr. Willis." He nodded some more, and said, "I'm puzzled. He was killed in your room. Did you give him permission to be in your room?"

"No."

"Well, do you have any idea what he might have been doing there?"

"He might have been looking for something to steal."

This time Regan was surprised; he wasn't faking the look he gave Parker. He said, "Steal? You mean Mr. Tiftus was a thief?"

"I wouldn't say that for sure. I heard rumors, around Miami."

"I see. Then would you say . . ."

The door opened, and two cops came in, and between them Tiftus' woman, Rhonda. Regan looked up, irritated, and one of the cops started to say something, and Rhonda took one look at Parker and screamed, "That's him! That's the bastard killed my husband! That's the one right there!"

Parker looked at her, and now he knew what Regan had gone away for: to set this up. He looked at Regan to see how it was supposed to play from here.

Regan was playing it to the hilt. He got to his feet and gave the cops stern looks and said, "Don't you know better than to barge in like that? I told you men to wait outside."

The woman kept hollering: "That's him! That's him!"

Regan said, "Get her out of here. What's the matter with you two?"

The cops didn't play their parts as well. They should have acted sheepish, or tried to apologize. Instead, they just turned the woman around and marched her back out again. She kept hollering till the door was shut.

Regan said, "I'm sorry about that."

Parker could play it open-face too, when he had to. He said, "Am I a suspect? I didn't realize that."

"No, I wouldn't exactly say you were a suspect, Mr. Willis. We are checking everything, of course, that's our job. By the way, do you mind? I don't mean to pry, but your face . . ."

Parker touched the side of his face where the shovel had hit him. It was still sensitive to the touch. "I fell down some stairs," he said. "Cellar stairs."

"I'm sorry to hear that. Recently?"

"This afternoon."

"Is that so? Did you have a doctor for it?"

"Yes. Dr. Rayborn, he's a local man."

Regan turned again to look at Younger, and said, "You know this Dr. Rayborn?"

"I'm the one sent for him."

Regan was surprised again, but he covered it better, this time. He said, "You were there?"

"Willis and I were in Joe Shardin's house when it happened."

"I see. Was this man Tiftus with you?"

"Tiftus?" Younger packed incredulity into the name. "What would he be doing with us?"

"I thought you all knew Shardin."

Parker broke in, saying, "I don't know about the captain, but I wasn't with Tiftus at all. He came to my room this morning, but I wouldn't waste any time on him and he went away."

"That was the last time you saw him?"

"I saw him on the street a little while later. We just said hello to each other."

"I see. That young lady seems to think you might have had a reason to kill Mr. Tiftus. Why would she think that, do you know?"

"No."

Regan waited, but Parker had nothing else to say. Off to the side, Younger fidgeted like he wanted to start talking, but he had sense enough to keep his mouth shut. Finally, Regan said, "Well, I suppose I'll find out when I hear her story." He looked at Younger again and said, "Have you known Mr. Willis long?"

"A couple of years," Younger said. "Joe Shardin introduced us, one time when Willis was up for a visit."

"I see." Regan tap-tap-tapped his fingers on Parker's wallet, still sitting on the desk. "Well," he said, "I guess that's about it for now, Mr. Willis. If I want to talk to you again later, you will be around, won't you? You weren't planning on leaving for Miami again right away, were you?"

"No. I'll be around a day or two anyway."

"That's fine. Thank you again for your co-operation."

Parker got to his feet, and took the wallet from the desk. "I won't be staying here at the hotel anymore," he said. "If you want me, you can get in touch with me at Joe Shardin's house. The captain has the address."

"Fine. Nice to have met you, Mr. Willis." He smiled as he said it, polite and friendly, but his eyes were watching Parker with flat professional curiosity, and he didn't get to his feet, and he didn't offer to shake hands. Just as Parker could smell law on Regan, Regan obviously could smell outlaw on Parker. He hadn't yet figured the connection between Parker and Younger, or whether or not either of them had had anything to do with killing Tiftus, but he did know something was out of kilter, and he looked the kind of cop who'd hang on until he found out what he wanted to know.

Younger stood up, too, but Regan said to him, "Why not stay for the rest of the interrogations, Abner? You can help me check the local details and whatnot, see I don't waste a lot of time on false trails."

Younger didn't like it, but he didn't have any choice. Sullen, he sat down again, and watched mistrustfully as Parker walked out of the office.

The next room was a smaller office, usually occupied by the manager's secretary. Tiftus' woman was in it now, with the two cops. Parker went over to her and said, "I didn't kill your man. I was with the fat cop when it happened. I'm clear."

The cops watched, blank-faced. The woman studied Parker's face and said, "I don't believe it. Who else around here would ease him the bump?"

Parker touched his face. "Same one who did this. Same tool."

One of the cops said, "I don't think you two ought to be talking."

"I'll be at Joe Shardin's place," Parker said, ignoring the cop. "When they're done with you, come over."

"What about what you did before?"

Parker knew what she meant; how much had he told the law himself? He said, "All I did before was tell your man to get lost when he came around to my room. I saw you with him in the lobby when he checked in, that's how come I knew who you were."

She shook her head doubtfully. "I'm not sure about you," she said. "I haven't made up my mind about you."

The cop said, "I think you two better quit now."

Parker looked at him. "You work for Regan or Younger?"

"Younger. It's Regan we're holding this lady for, but we're city officers."

"You better check with Younger before you tell Regan I stopped here to talk with the lady."

The cop frowned. "How come?"

"You know what Younger thinks of Regan," Parker

said, because it couldn't be a secret. "Younger wants to keep what he knows to himself this time."

The cop shrugged. "I'll check with him," he said.

"That's good." Parker nodded at the woman. "See you later, Rhonda," he said.

She seemed surprised he'd remembered her name.

4

Parker opened the door and said, "Come on in, Rhonda."

She came in with the belligerent air of a dumb woman afraid something's being put over on her. She said, "What's with you and that Captain Younger? He's a cop, ain't he?"

"That's right." He shut the door and led the way into the living room. "Sit down."

"I want something to drink."

"In the kitchen."

"Oh, a real gentleman."

Parker turned to look at her. "We don't have much time before Younger gets here," he said.

"So what's that to me?"

Parker shook his head. She wanted to be snotty, and there was no reason for her to be snotty. He said, "Whatever the drag is here, you inherit Tiftus' cut. Don't that mean anything to you?"

"How come I'm in? You kept throwing my man out,

but me you let in. What is this, be kind to widows week?"

"Your name ain't Tiftus."

"Thank God it ain't. What do you want from me, buster? You figure to move in now my man's gone?"

"No," Parker told her, and it was the truth. He had a woman in Miami for one thing, and for another he was working. This wasn't his usual kind of work, but it had the same smell to it, and when he was working he had no time for women. Before and after, but not during.

She cocked her head and studied him, trying to decide if he was telling the truth or not. She finally shrugged and said, "Okay, so much for my sex appeal. You already seen me naked so now you don't want any more. If that ain't it, what do you want?"

"I want to know the game."

"The what?"

Parker said, "Tiftus came here looking for something. Younger's looking for it. Whoever killed Tiftus is looking for it. Everybody figures I got the inside track on where it is, but I don't."

"Why not?"

"I don't know *what* it is."

She opened her eyes wide and looked at him. "You don't?"

"It has something to do with Joe Sheer, but I don't know what."

"Who the hell is Joe Sheer?"

Parker pointed at the floor. "You're in his house."

"I thought that was Shardin. It was Shardin in the phone book, that's how I found the place."

"He changed his name. The question is, did Tiftus tell you what he was looking for?"

"Sure."

"What?"

"Money," she said, as though it were the most obvious thing in the world.

"Yeah, but how? Cash? Jewelry? Goods of some kind?"

She shrugged. "Beats me," she said. "Money is all I know. He said we were coming here to make us a hundred G's or maybe more."

Parker said, "From Joe Sheer? Joe Shardin?"

"You got me, buster. All I know is what I told you."

"He never said anything about Joe."

"Not one word. He never said anything about anybody, except you. He seen you, when we went in the lobby, and he said, 'Oh oh, there's somebody else standing in line. I know that bo.' And as soon as we checked in he went to see you."

Parker shook his head. "Go make yourself that drink," he said.

"You're a real sport," she said, and went on into the kitchen.

Parker went over by the window and looked out. That teenage kid was on the porch next door again, looking in this direction. All this activity, people going in and out of a dead man's house, it was going to get all the neighbors looking after a while. This thing couldn't drag on much longer.

But he couldn't seem to learn anything. Tiftus had come here looking for a hundred thousand dollars, maybe more, but there was no way to tell what the hundred thousand looked like right now. It could be cash, or it could be jewelry. It could even be a few paintings stolen from museums, works of art, precious documents of one kind or another. A hundred thousand dollars could be in a lot of different shapes, a lot of different colors.

What about the woman? Maybe she was the one killed Tiftus herself, and maybe she knew the whole story and was keeping it to herself.

Except it hadn't been Tiftus down in that cellar, and it hadn't been the woman, and it hadn't been Younger. There was someone else involved, ready to kill, in too damn much of a hurry to kill.

It didn't feel like a professional. The way he'd got himself cornered in the cellar and the way he'd got out of it again, both of them smacked like the doings of an impulsive amateur. Same with the killing; cutting Tiftus down hadn't solved anything or proved anything. All he'd done by killing Tiftus was alert all the law for miles around, make it that much tougher on himself and everybody else.

So it was an amateur, probably somebody local. Dr. Rayborn? Or Gliffe, the undertaker? Parker didn't know enough about either, or know how much either of them knew. He'd have to talk to Younger about them.

In the meantime, there were other things to do. He turned away from the window and went out to the kitchen. The woman was there searching the cabinets. She looked startled when Parker came in, and then frightened, and then innocent. The last expression didn't work too well.

Parker said, "I'll take care of that."

"I was looking for swizzle sticks," she said.

He said, "You go sit in the living room, keep a watch out front. When Younger shows up, you let me know and then get out the back way without him seeing you. Go on back to the hotel, and I'll get in touch with you."

"What are you gonna do, search the place?"

"Look for swizzle sticks."

"And I inherit, huh?"

"That's right."

"Huh. I'll believe it when I see it."

But she went on into the living room, and Parker went to work.

5

Younger came in and said, "That Regan's a pain in the ass. I'll put a complaint in on him, I swear to Christ I will."

"What does he think about us?" Parker asked him.

"What the hell do I care? I'm running that goddam show, not him."

"Sure." Parker shut the door.

Younger said, "What did you say to that Samuels woman?"

"Who?"

"Your partner's girlfriend. Rhonda Samuels. She clammed up the second time she came in, said it was all a mistake, you looked like somebody else, she didn't mean it anyway. What did you say to her?"

"Nothing. Come on in the living room."

They went into the living room, and Younger said, "I've been thinking."

"Yeah?"

"The guy that killed your partner, he's the same one hit you, the one that was digging in the cellar."

That was too obvious to answer. Parker lit a cigarette and went over by the front window. The Harold Teen was gone from the next-door porch.

Younger said, "That means he didn't find it, you see that? If it was buried in the cellar and he'd found it, he would of took off with it, right? He wouldn't still be around, he wouldn't of killed your partner."

Parker said, "What if Regan gets to him?" Looking out the window he saw Tiftus' woman go across the front lawn to the sidewalk and walk away. She'd done it the dumb way, but it had worked out; Younger couldn't see her from where he was sitting.

Younger said, "You mean, before I do? Don't worry about it, Willis, I'm still in charge. Regan can throw his weight around, I let him get away with it, but when the chips are down I'm still the one in charge. If the killer's found, he'll be turned over right away to me. I'll have him in one of my own cells, don't you worry about a thing."

"What about that doctor, Rayborn? And Gliffe?"

Younger frowned. "What about them?"

"They're in this. What if it's one of them, the guy that killed Tiftus?"

But Younger shook his head. "Not them, not either of them. They don't know anything about this, Willis."

"They're in it up to their ears. Gliffe called you when I went to see him. You called Rayborn to keep me at his place."

"They don't know anything about the money."

Younger seemed sure of himself, but he was always sure of himself. Parker said, "Check them out. Find out where they were when I was clubbed in this house here and when Tiftus was killed."

Younger shrugged. "All right, I'll do it, but it isn't either one of them, I guarantee it."

"Fine. Let's get to business." Parker went over and sat down in an armchair. Now was the time to get the full story. He said, "Where do you think it's hidden? In the house?" He already knew it wasn't; while waiting for Younger, he'd finished up the searching he'd started earlier in the day. He'd looked in the cellar and found nothing but the half-dug hole, and then he'd searched the attic, which was hot and filthy and low-ceilinged and just about empty. It looked as though Joe himself had never been up there, but Parker had gone over it anyway and found nothing but dust.

Still, he tossed the suggestion at Younger, to push the idea of his own ignorance, and Younger tossed it back: "Not here," he said. "Take my word for it, Willis, that money isn't in this house. All the old bastard kept in here was a thousand bucks in the flour canister, and I already got that."

Parker covered his surprise, and said, "How'd you find that?"

"Don't you worry, Willis, I'm not as dumb as you think I am. Or as Joe Sheer thought I was, either. I know what's going on."

"Yeah. So you figure there's still a hundred thousand hidden away somewhere, but not in . . ."

"A hundred thousand? That's low, Willis, that's so low it's funny. You don't know as much as you think you do."

"I don't? Then how much?"

"Hidden away?" Younger sat forward on the sofa, leaning over in a confidential way, and half whispered, "The way I figure it, it has to be at least half a million. Maybe more."

Parker looked at him. Half a million, in cash? Joe Sheer had never had half a million bucks in his life, for one thing, and if he ever had that much dough he wouldn't have hidden it somewhere in cash. There were better things to do with money, safer and more useful.

The whole thing had to be a pipe-dream. Tiftus, Younger, the third guy whoever he was, all after the wild goose. Tiftus was stupid enough, and Younger was greedy enough, and the third guy was amateur enough.

If all this trouble was coming out of a bedtime story, it was too much.

Parker shook his head; he still couldn't believe it. He had to know for sure. He said, "Spell it out for me, Younger. Show me how it adds up that high."

"Well, it just figures," Younger told him, like a man explaining his religion. "It figures, that's all. It's bound to be anyway that much. Anyway that much."

"Show me."

"I will. I will." Younger pulled a legal-size envelope from his inside coat pocket and waved it in the air, saying, "I worked out the numbers on it, I worked it out all the way down the line."

"Let's see."

"Well, just look. Come on over here and look."

Younger pulled some papers from the envelope and unfolded it. It was two sheets of large-size blank stationery, written on with pen and ink in a cramped and spidery script. Younger spread the sheets out on the coffee table and said, "Come over here and look."

Parker went over and sat on the sofa and looked. On the first sheet, the one Younger was pointing at, there was a long list, three items across. The first was a year, the second the name of a city, the third a number in the thousands. The list started off

1915	Louisville	12,000
1915	Sacramento	14,500
1916	Troy, N.Y.	9,000

It went on that way, a long, long list, and down at the bottom of the page the numbers on the right had been totaled up, and the final sum written in: 1,876,000.

Except for that final number, Parker recognized the handwriting; it was Joe Sheer's. And the number at the bottom of the page, would that be Captain Younger's writing?

Younger was saying, "See, this is Joe Sheer's history, every robbery he was ever connected with, right from when he started in 1915 right up till when he retired. See, that's the date, and that's the city where the robbery was, and that's how much he got out of it. His cut, see? And down there at the bottom, that's how much he earned over his whole lifetime, almost two million dollars. That's a hell of a lot of money, isn't it? Almost two million dollars. Fifty-seven robberies in forty-three years. Almost two million dollars."

Parker nodded. It was what he'd thought; a fable. "What next?" he said.

"Simple arithmetic," Younger told him. "Just simple figuring, that's all."

"Show me."

Younger's hands were covering the second sheet of paper. He said, "Such as, how much do you figure he spent a year? He made a lot of money, right, but how much do you think he spent? He had to be careful, not be too noticeable so people would wonder where his money came from, so what do you think? Twenty-five thousand a year? Maybe not even that much."

"Maybe more," Parker told him.

But Younger shook his head, sure of his ground. "On what?" he wanted to know. "How the hell can you spend more than twenty-five thousand dollars a year? It's impossible. Unless you're a millionaire already, everybody knows it and you got nothing to worry about. But somebody like Joe Sheer? He wouldn't dare spend too much. Twenty-five thousand a year is figuring *high*. Willis, believe me."

Parker didn't believe him. He spent more than

twenty-five thousand a year himself, and so had Joe for most of his life. But Younger was at a different level; he'd never had twenty-five thousand dollars all to himself in one year, so he couldn't understand what could be done with money.

Younger took his hands away from the second sheet. "All right," he said. "Here's the figures."

There were more numbers on this second sheet, but they weren't what caught Parker's eye. Besides the numbers there was a list of names, scattered down the right side of the paper. Loomis, McKay, Parker, Littlefield, Clinger . . . a long, long list of thirty or more names, all of them men Joe Sheer had worked with at one time or another.

But not in Joe's handwriting. The list of names, and the figures over on the other side of the page, were all done in the same handwriting as the total on the first sheet.

Younger looked up, smiling his smug smile, tapping a finger against the list of names. "See that there? It wouldn't surprise me none if your name's down there. Don't think I ever bought that Willis name."

Parker looked at him, seeing him definitely for the first time as a dead man. "Let's get on with it," he said.

Younger's smile faded. Looking at Parker, his eyes began to get a little uncertain. He lowered his head, cleared his throat, and tapped the sheet of paper. "This is it, here," he said. "Never mind that other stuff, that doesn't matter. This is what matters."

Parker waited.

Tracing the numbers with his fingers, Younger said, "Sheer made one million, eight hundred seventy-six thousand dollars, right? In forty-three years. Now, we figure he spent twenty-five thousand a year, forty-three years, that's a million and seventy-five thousand dollars. You subtract that from what he made, you got eight hundred and one thousand dollars left over. Eight hundred thousand he never spent, Willis!"

Parker nodded. It was a pretty castle Younger had in the air there.

Younger said, "Sheer showed me some bankbooks and mutual fund records and other stuff like that, just about a hundred and twenty thousand bucks worth. That's the money he had out in the open, to explain what he was living on. But the rest he had hidden away. He had to; he couldn't have explained it otherwise, see? A hundred and twenty thousand from eight hundred thousand, that's six hundred and eighty thousand dollars left over! You see it, Willis? Six hundred and eighty thousand dollars! Even if he was spending like crazy the last five years, buying this house and all, there's still got to be at least half a million left, at *least* half a million! And that's a conservative estimate, Willis, a conservative estimate! Way back in 1915, 1916, he didn't spend any twenty-five thousand a year *then*, not by a long shot. There may be even more than half a million left."

Parker got to his feet. It was the way he'd thought. Tiftus had figured Joe's goods closer to the truth, but Tiftus, too, hadn't been able to think more sensibly than a box of dough stashed away somewhere. That was what Tiftus would do, hide it in a mattress or bury it in the ground out by the old oak tree, but Joe Sheer had more sense; he invested it, in safe stocks and good mutual funds, and let the money work for him.

Parker lit a cigarette, and walked around the room, back and forth. He said, "You talked to Joe Sheer about this, huh?"

"Sure I did. Where you think I got all these figures?" Younger picked up the two sheets of paper again and folded them to put back in the envelope. "And the names," he said. "The figures and the names, all straight from Sheer."

"When you told him about the half million, what did he say?"

Younger smiled, remembering. "He tried to give me a lot of crap, Willis," he said. "Just like you tried once or twice."

"What did he say?"

"He said he'd spent it all. He said the hundred and twenty thousand was all he had left."

"But you don't think so."

"Come off it, Willis. Let me give you the proof. I put a little pressure on him, and he came up with the thousand bucks from the flour canister. Not only that, he told me he'd give me the whole hundred and twenty thousand, he'd write letters off and get it all back from the mutual funds and everywhere and give me the whole damn thing. Now, would he give me all that if he didn't have a hell of a lot more stashed away some-where else?"

Parker nodded, seeing the whole thing.

Younger said, "If he hadn't of died, I'd of found out where the rest of it was."

That was a surprise. It meant Younger hadn't killed Joe after all. But Younger was still the trouble Joe had talked about in the letters, the trouble that had made Joe a stupid old man.

Everything, Joe had given Younger everything, his history, his friends, his savings, and all he'd done was make Younger want more. It was a good thing Joe died when he did, before he started giving Younger his friends' addresses.

Younger said, "So I'm not the hick cop you thought I was, huh?"

Parker looked at him and shook his head. "No," he said.

"There's half a million," Younger said. "Half a mil-lion hidden away somewhere. Isn't there, Willis? Isn't there?"

If it wasn't for the Willis name, he'd kill Younger right now and clear out of here. But there was Regan to think about, and the Willis name. Until this whole mess got cleared up, the only thing to do was to play along with Younger. Grab the ball and run. He nodded and said, "There's half a million. Sheer was lying to you."

"I know damn well he was. And we'll find that

dough, won't we? There's enough for both of us, and we'll find it."

"Sure we will," Parker told him.

Younger smiled, a big fat happy beaming round toothy stupid smile. "Sure we will," he said.

PART THREE

1

Abner L. Younger was nobody's fool. He'd been around. Thirty-seven states and fourteen foreign lands including Germany, Japan, England, and the Canal Zone. When a man spends thirty years in the United States Army, he doesn't come out of it a hick, no sir. He comes out of it knowing what's what.

Younger had had some sort of title in front of his name for almost as long as he could remember. At twenty, a green frightened dumb kid from the hick town of Sagamore, in Nebraska, he'd become Private Abner L. Younger, USA. That was the time of the Great Depression; there was no work for Abner's father anywhere to be found, and if there was no work for the father there was sure as hell no work for the son. If he wanted three meals every day and a bed indoors every night, the only thing in the world for Abner to do was join the Army.

Promotion came slow both sides of the ocean in those days, and when the Second World War came along in 1941 Younger had advanced only one small step, up to a Pfc. But with the war came promotions for everybody, and soft jobs for those who'd been smart enough to be in the Army already when the war started. Younger spent his wartime service at a basic training camp, and wound up a buck sergeant when the war was over.

He had twenty years of duty behind him a few years later, and could have retired then, but he'd just got another promotion, and knew he had a good chance to make master sergeant by the time thirty years was up, which would mean a hell of a lot more pension, so he decided to stick it out the extra ten.

He made master sergeant. Almost anybody can, if he stays in the Army long enough. Then his thirty years were done, and while he was going through the discharge red tape a clerk asked him what his civilian address was going to be.

And he didn't know. Neither of his parents was still alive, and he'd been out of touch with any other relatives for decades. He finally told the clerk General Delivery, Sagamore, Nebraska, as a temporary address, because he couldn't think of anything else. He'd forward a permanent address when he had one.

That was the only reason he went back to Sagamore, to pick up his pension checks. But once there, there was no reason to leave, nowhere else to go, no one anywhere in the world that he wanted to see or that wanted to see him. So he stayed on. He joined the local American Legion Post, and through that got to know some of the better element in town, and settled down to enjoy his retirement.

But he was only fifty. He'd had something to do all his life, donning a uniform every day and going to a specific place and having specific things to do. Time hung heavy, now he was retired. He had no hobbies, and his pension wasn't lavish. He found he was lying around the house late in the mornings, and going too often to the movies, and spending too much time in front of the television set either at home or down at the bar in the cellar of the American Legion Post. He was drinking too much beer, eating badly, getting too little exercise. He was putting on weight, and his digestion was going bad.

Then the police job came along. He heard talk about it down at the American Legion, about old Captain Greene retiring and wonder who'll take over, there's no men with good leadership qualities on the force at all. The pay's too low to attract first-rate men, somebody said, and that led straight into the old argument about property taxes, but Younger had heard enough.

So now he had the highest rank of all. Not Private Younger anymore, not Pfc Younger, not even Master Sergeant Younger. *Captain* Younger. Yes, and it could just as well be General Younger, because he was the highest-ranking man on the force. Seventeen men, and he was their captain.

At first he wore the uniform all the time, dark blue with modified riding pants, and boots and a garrison cap. But the weight he'd put on never came off again, and he had to admit he didn't look good in the uniform. Besides, R.H.I.P. Rank Has Its Privileges. As captain, he could wear civvies if he wanted. As captain, he was the only man on the force who could wear civvies. So he started wearing civvies.

But that made a problem. In the uniform, he was declaring his rank for the whole world to see, but in civvies what was he but just another stocky civilian? He thought about it and thought about it, and finally settled on the cowboy hat. A good ten-gallon hat would set him apart, announce to the world that here was a man who held *some* rank, that was for sure. A cowboy hat and a good suit, the combination would show he was something special. Besides, he thought he looked good dressed that way.

At fifty-one, he'd reached the peak. Captain of the Police Department, a respected citizen, secretary of the American Legion Post; he was content, he had everything he wanted.

And then he was shown the possibility of wanting a lot more.

It happened almost by accident. In his first months on the force, Younger was working all the time. He revamped the files, worked out a new shift rotation for the men, started correspondence with the county sheriff's office and various state police offices, and decided to familiarize himself with everyone in town. He wanted to be able to know, just from looking at a man, if he was local or a stranger. If he was local, Younger

wanted to know everything there was to know about
him; what he did for a living, if he was married or not, if
he owned his own home, if he'd ever been in trouble.

Sagamore was a small town, and a dull one. Trou-
blemakers and other lively types left early, and didn't
come back. As a result, making up a mental card file
on the town wasn't very hard, or very interesting, except for one man, one citizen who stood out from all
the rest.

Joseph T. Shardin.

The facts about Shardin were few. He owned his
home, he was retired, he'd lived in town about five
years. He made frequent trips down to Omaha, staying
a day or two or sometimes up to a week, and every
once in a great while he had a visitor or two at his
house, always strangers from out of town. He didn't
have any relatives around here, and no one had ever
seen him before he'd come here to retire.

Beyond that, it was all a blank. Younger couldn't
find out exactly what Shardin had retired from. At the
bank he learned Shardin had a banking account, and
kept it supplied by depositing checks that were divi-
dends on investments or payments on life-insurance
policies or Social Security dribbles. But no pension
check, from a company or the government, no income
to suggest what kind of work he'd done before retiring.

Younger got more and more interested. He wasn't
suspicious at first, just stretching a bit in his new job.
He was running a police force, and here was a chance

to do a bit of detective work, unravel a mystery. He did it for fun, more than anything else.

Not learning much from the people around Shardin, Younger next tried to learn from Shardin himself. He coached one of his patrolmen, a youngster with an honest, stupid face, and sent him off to see Shardin as a census taker. Among the questions about age and sex and how many occupants in the house, he also asked about Shardin's background: place of birth, principal occupation, most recent employer, last three addresses. Shardin, according to the patrolman's report, answered all the questions easily and calmly, and didn't suspect a thing.

The only thing wrong, the answers didn't check out.

For place of birth, Shardin had put Harrisburg, Pennsylvania. Younger wrote to Harrisburg, asking for information on a Joseph T. Shardin, born in their city on January 12, 1894. They wrote back there was no record of a Joseph T. Shardin born in their city on that or any other date.

For principal occupation, Shardin had put sports promoter, explaining he had promoted boxing matches, wrestling, roller-derbies, stock-car races, and other sports events in the east, mostly Pennsylvania and New York. Younger wrote to both the Pennsylvania and New York Boxing Commissions, and both wrote back they had no record of any Joseph T. Shardin.

For most recent employer, Shardin had put Midstate Arena Attractions, Inc., Scranton, Pennsylvania. Younger wrote a letter to this company, asking for in-

formation on Shardin, and the letter came back with a
post office rubber stamp on the envelope: ADDRESSEE
UNKNOWN.

All three former addresses Shardin had given were
false.

Younger was now sure he'd found a wrong one.
Shardin had an income from unknown sources, chose
to live in a place where he wasn't known, and gave a
false background.

The next time Shardin went to Omaha, Captain
Younger, with a skeleton key, went into Shardin's
house. In the kitchen he set up his fingerprint equip-
ment, the learning about which had been another part
of his early enthusiasm for the new job, and from the
water glasses in the kitchen cabinet he got three perfect fingerprints. He set up his camera and his white
cardboard backdrop, and took three pictures of each
print, just to be on the safe side. Then he cleaned up
the traces of his having been there, and went back to
the station to have the film developed. He mailed a set
of the photos to Washington with a covering letter that
gave no details but simply asked for whatever identification and information he could get about the owner
of those prints, and then there was nothing to do but
wait.

A week later a phone call came from the Federal
agency office in Omaha. "About a set of fingerprints
you sent Washington about a week ago."

"What about them?"

But the Federal man was calling to ask questions,

not to answer them. He said, "What was that inquiry in connection with, Captain?"

Younger felt a sudden transitory dread; had he stumbled on some sort of secret government agent? Was Shardin actually a counter-spy or something? If he was, the government wouldn't like some hick cop poking around after their man, causing a ruckus.

But that couldn't be it. Shardin was an old man of seventy; what kind of secret agent was that? Besides, why would the government establish an undercover man for five years in a nothing little town like Sagamore?

The Federal man had been waiting for an answer. He said, "Are you there, Captain?"

"What? Yes, yes, of course, I was just looking for the folder . . ." He already had his story worked out, just in case he was asked this question, and all he had to do now was get his wits collected and tell it. He said, "We had a little burglary here, a liquor store ransacked. We checked the place out for fingerprints, and those three were the only ones we couldn't match to somebody we already knew was in the store that day."

"A liquor store robbery. Odd."

Younger held the phone so tightly that afterwards his hand ached. "Who is it?" he asked. "Who do they belong to?"

"Man named Joseph Sheer. I'm only—"

"How do you spell that?"

The Federal man spelled it, and then said, "It's a

surprise to hear from him. We thought he was dead by now."

"Oh? An old man, huh?"

"He'd be about seventy now."

"Seventy years old. What's the story on him? He wanted for anything?"

"There's four Federal warrants out on him, all for bank robbery. But the most recent is back in '53. He's gone downhill since then, if he's breaking into liquor stores. A rummy now, I guess. Most of them end up that way."

"I guess they do," Younger said. "Where was this bank robbery, the one back in '53?"

"Cleveland. You'll be getting a full report in the mail, from Washington."

"Thanks for calling," Younger said.

"If you happen to get him," the Federal man said, making it clear he didn't believe Younger ever would, "be sure to let us know."

"Oh, I will," Younger promised. "Thanks again," he said, and hung up.

After he'd hung up, it occurred to him he should have told the Federal man the truth. "I know where Joe Sheer is," he should have said. "I'll go pick him up and hold him for you," he should have said. Why didn't he?

This was just a little hobby, a little sidelight, a little piece of amateur detecting. When it turned up a wanted criminal, why didn't he right away make the arrest? Why had he readied that phoney liquor store yarn in advance?

He knew why. He'd known why all along, without thinking it out in plain words. Money was the reason. He'd looked at Joseph T. Shardin, and he'd seen something out of kilter, and he'd sensed an advantage to himself, and he smelled money in it, profit in it somehow. Money, more money than he'd ever even thought about before. More money than he'd made in all his thirty years in the Army put together, *plus* his pension from now till the day he died. So much money, so much. . . . He didn't know how much, he couldn't even guess.

But he could ask.

Abner L. Younger, after fifty-one years of life having at last found the vocation he'd been born for, put on his cowboy hat and went off to talk to a fella *really* named Joe Sheer.

2

Younger smiled and stepped across the threshold and said, "Just a routine call, Mr. Shardin. I'm Captain Younger."

The old man hesitated, still holding the door open even though Younger was already in the house. He said, "Routine? What do you mean, routine? Who are you?"

Younger's smile was affable, apologetic, self-assured. "Oh, I'm sorry," he said, but he didn't sound it. "Police department. Captain Abner L. Younger, Sagamore Police Department."

A film seemed to come down over the old man's eyes, a thin veneer of caution and watchfulness. He was well-preserved, thin but healthy-looking, with leathery flesh on face and hands, teeth too discolored to be false, and a full head of hair mottled grey and white. He was probably taller than the captain, but age had stooped him and he was now an inch or so shorter.

Younger, still smiling, nodding his head in satisfaction with the world in general, strolled on into the living room, saying, "Very nice place you've got here, Mr. Shardin, very nice. The old Hoyt place, isn't it?"

The old man followed him. "I suppose so. The people I bought it from were named Hoyt."

"You've certainly fixed it up nice for yourself. Looks real cozy."

The old man said, "What's this about, Captain?" The voice had overtones of impatience and irritation.

Younger ignored the overtones. "Just routine," he said airily, and made a vague gesture with his hands. "No hurry," he said. He took off his cowboy hat, twirled it in his hands, and gazed fondly around the room.

"I was working in my garden," the old man said pointedly. "I'd like to get back to it while there's still daylight."

"A garden?" Happy surprise lighting his face, Younger put the cowboy hat back on his head and said, "You've got to show it to me. Would you believe it, I've always wanted a garden, but traveling around all the— No, don't show me, I can find the way."

The old man hadn't made any move to show Younger the way. He stood there and watched Younger go by, headed towards the kitchen and the back door, and there was nothing for him to do but follow.

Younger had never been in the house before, but he had no trouble finding his way around it. There were maybe hundreds of thousands of dollars hidden somewhere on this property, and Younger was determined to know what the property looked like. He'd got the house plan on file at the assessor's office, and now he was making a physical survey.

He was also taking the first step in the campaign he'd decided to use against Joe Sheer. A frontal attack wouldn't do him any good, he had sense enough to realize that, so a more oblique method was called for. He was pleased with the method he'd decided on.

He went through the kitchen now, and out the back door, and had his first look at Joe Sheer's garden. Was the money hidden there, buried in the garden? Or hidden away in the house somewhere?

It might not be here at all. It might be down in Omaha, wherever Sheer lived down there. But Sheer spent a lot more time at this place here than he did in Omaha, so wasn't it more likely this was where he kept the money?

The old man had followed him out of the house. Younger turned to him and said, "That's a really beautiful garden you have there, Mr. Shardin. Shardin? Is that the right pronunciation?"

The old man looked startled for just a second, but then he recovered and nodded briefly and said, "You've got it right."

"Well." Younger squinted up at the afternoon sun, glanced at his wristwatch, looked around again at the garden, and said, "Well, you want to get back to what you were doing. I won't keep you any longer."

The old man frowned. "You're going?"

"No need to show me through the house, I can go

around the side here. Nice to have met you, Mr. Shardin." He started away, around the side of the house.

The old man took a few steps after him, saying, "What did you want? What did you come here for?"

"Just routine," Younger called, and waved, and walked on out to the sidewalk.

3

As the train was pulling away from the station, Younger slid into the empty seat beside the old man. "Well, well! Fancy meeting you here? Going down into the city?"

The old man had been looking out of the window at the station, sunk in his own thoughts. He turned, startled, and for a few seconds didn't say anything. When at last he did speak, all he said was, "Oh. It's you."

"I certainly did enjoy our little chat the other day," Younger told him. "I want to get to know all the folks that moved into town while I was away. I was in the Army, you know."

Younger's silence forced the old man to say something; he chose, "I didn't know that."

"Thirty years," Younger told him, and nodded emphatically. "Retired a master sergeant. Just a few months ago, just retired, came back to the old home town, took over the police force, whipping it into shape. You've been in town just about five years, haven't you?"

"Yes."

"A fine town. You get down into the city often?"

"Sometimes."

Younger already knew about that. He'd followed the old man on his last trip in, before starting this campaign. He knew now about the old man's apartment in town. Sheer had stayed there two days that last time, and the second day he'd had visitors, three stocky men about Younger's age. They'd driven up in a Plymouth with New York State plates, stayed the afternoon and evening, left about eleven-thirty at night. Younger had copied the license number down, but hadn't done anything about it. Time enough if it was necessary.

What he figured, he figured those three men were bank robbers, too. Maybe Joe Sheer was retired, and then again maybe he wasn't. Maybe these days he just drew up the plans for the robberies, let the younger men actually go in and do the jobs. Younger would find out, in time. He'd know everything there was to know, in time.

They rode in silence a while now, until Younger took out a cigar and began to unwrap it. A sign at the front end of the car said no smoking was allowed here, but Younger went on unwrapping the cigar, tossed the paper on the floor, stuck the cigar in his mouth, and reached for a match. Just before lighting it, he turned to the old man, saying, "That's the advantage of being a policeman." He grinned and winked.

The old man looked at him with distaste. "What is?"

Younger gestured at the no-smoking sign. "You can bend the law a little," he said. He lit the cigar, puffed a halo of smoke, and tossed the match on the floor. "Now, you," he said, "if you were to bend the law, we'd get you. Sooner or later we'd get you, even if it took twenty years."

The old man said nothing at that, and they rode in silence again until Younger said, "Were you ever in the Army?"

"No." The old man seemed about to stop there, but then he apparently had to justify himself. He added, "I failed the physical in the First War."

"That's too bad. The Army's a great life, great life."

"Maybe so."

Younger started telling war stories then. He told the old man story after story about his Army days, some of them true, some borrowed, and some embroidered, some completely false. The old man listened stolidly, never speaking, sometimes looking out the window at the flat scenery going by, and Younger talked on and on and on.

When they arrived in Omaha, Younger walked with the old man out of the terminal. On the way, he said, "How long you staying in town?"

The old man shrugged. "A couple of days."

"Maybe we'll ride back together." Younger smiled, happy and friendly.

The old man gave him a cold and thoughtful look, and then looked away. "Maybe we will," he said.

"I wouldn't be a bit surprised," Younger said.

Neither of them were.

4

Well, hello!"

The old man had just stepped out of the supermarket, a bag of groceries in his hands. He looked up and saw Younger standing there, and a shadow crossed his face. All at once he seemed ten years older.

Younger said, "That looks heavy. I'm going your way, I'll give you a lift."

"No, that's all right, I—"

"No trouble at all." Younger took the bag of groceries and started away with them, and the old man couldn't do a thing but follow.

The police car was parked at the curb. Younger usually drove his own car, a small black Ford, but especially for today he'd borrowed the department's brand-new squad car, a green-and-yellow car with a red dome light on the roof, a whip antenna on the left side, and the word POLICE in huge yellow letters on hood and trunk and both doors.

"Here we are." Younger put the bag of groceries on the back seat, then held the front door open for the old man, who hesitated a dangerous fraction of a second before getting in. For just an instant there, Joe Sheer might have gone on the offensive, but the instant passed. Younger smiled at the old man's back, then slammed the door and strode around the car to the other side and got behind the wheel.

The car was even more official-looking inside than out. The usual chrome-filled dashboard was supplemented by additional knobs for the dome light, and siren and spotlight, plus the two-way radio, plus a clipboard held to the top of the dash by a small magnet. The radio was switched on, breathing static and occasionally breaking into guttural voice.

There were seat belts in the car, and Younger made a production of fastening his, though he usually ignored such things. To the old man he said, "Better fasten your belt too, Joe. Safety first, right? You always want to be able to feel you're safe, isn't that right?"

His voice flat, the old man said, "I suppose so." He fastened his seat belt with a click.

Younger started the car, and they glided silently through the traffic, sunlight glinting off the polished hood. After a minute, Younger laughed and said, "What'll your friends think, huh, Joe? Anybody sees you go by in a police car, they'll say, 'Well, what do you know? The cops caught up with old Joe at last.' You'll have a lot of explaining to do, Joe." He laughed some more, and shook his head at how funny it was.

The old man said, "What do you want, Captain? What do you want from me?"

Younger hesitated, but the time wasn't ripe. He'd only been working a couple of weeks on this, and Sheer was still too tough. He'd be asking that question again some other time, with a lot less challenge in his voice. So this time all Younger said was, "I'll take a cup of coffee, Joe, but that's all. If I let you pay me to drive you home, the cabbies'd all be after me." He laughed, and winked, and jabbed his elbow into the old man's arm.

Sheer kept looking at him, as though he were going to say something else, but after a minute he sat back and looked out at the traffic, and another dangerous moment had passed.

Two blocks later they passed a house with a FOR SALE sign out on the front lawn. Younger pointed at it and said, "I know those folks, and they're crazy. You know that, Joe?"

The old man frowned. "Are they?"

"Sure they are. To sell a house now, move out of town like they're doing, it just doesn't make any sense. The timing's all wrong for it, the market's off in houses and the whole thing is just a terrible loss all the way around." He shook his head. "I would tell anybody, Joe, right now is the worst time in the world to think about moving. Absolutely disastrous, Joe." He laughed and said, "Why, I wouldn't even go away for a *visit* right now. No, sir. This is a time to stay put right here in good old Sagamore. You know what I mean, Joe?"

The old man said, "I know what you mean." Already there was a bit less toughness in his voice.

5

Younger sat in his office and looked at the telephone. Call now? Or wait a little longer?

He hadn't seen the old man for three days now. He had the old man worried, had him knowing Younger was watching him for something or other, and now he just pulled back a little bit, sat back, let the old man start to sweat. That was all, just give him time to sweat, time to think.

And then come in again all of a sudden, and this time cut just a little bit deeper than before.

Now.

He picked up the phone and dialed Sheer's number from memory. This was the first time he'd ever telephoned the old man, but he knew his number by heart. He knew the old man backward and forward.

The phone rang four times, and then the old man picked the receiver up and said "Hello?"

"Hello, Joe? Joe Shardin?"

"Speaking," the old man said doubtfully, as though he thought he recognized the voice.

Not that Younger had meant to keep it a secret. He identified himself right away, saying, "This is Captain Younger, Joe. I'm sorry to disturb you this way, I really am. I wouldn't do it for the world if it wasn't absolutely necessary."

"What is it this time, Captain?" The old man's voice was cold as ice.

"This won't take long, Joe, I've just got to check for our records. I believe we've got the wrong spelling of your name down here, and I figured the best thing was just to check with you. Now, what it says here, it says S-H-E-E-R-D-I-N. Now, that isn't right, is it, Joe?"

There was silence on the line.

Younger said, "Joe? Are you there, Joe?"

"What do you *want*, Younger?"

"Is that the way you spell your name or isn't it? Joe, there's no need to get touchy about this, all I want—"

"You know how I spell my name!"

"Well, let me just make sure I've got it straight here, I wouldn't want to—"

"You'd better cut this out, Younger. If you know what's good for you—"

"Joe? Is that you? What the hell are you talking like that for, Joe?"

"You know what I'm talking about, you son of a bitch, I'm talk—"

"Joe, you never talked like that to my face. Is that

the way you felt about me all along? And here I thought we were friends, Joe. We always talked together so easy, there was never any secrets between us, no hard feelings—"

"This is harassment, Younger, that's what it is. You don't think I know the law?" The old man was making an obvious attempt at self-control; his voice trembled with the need to shout, but did not shout. "I'll get me a lawyer, you son of a bitch, I'll have you—"

Younger said, pouring his voice into the telephone like maple syrup, "You want to make a formal complaint against me, Joe? You sure that's what you want? You'd have to come down here to the station, if that's what you wanted, Joe. It's cold down here, you know that? Cold and hard, with bars on the windows, not nice and warm and soft and comfy like you got at home. You got old bones, Joe, old bones and old skin and old blood; you sure you want to come down to this place?"

"You can't get away with this. I know my rights. This is harassment; you can't get away with it." But the trembling in the old man's voice was more pronounced now, and from a different cause.

Younger said, "The way you get all excited, Joe, over nothing at all, somebody might think you had something to hide. That's no way to carry on."

"If you think you've got something on me, then why don't you *do* something about it?"

Younger smiled into the phone, and let a few seconds go by before he answered, seconds for the old man to hear what he'd just said, hear the echo of his own words, hear what they sounded like. Then he said, "What do you suggest, Joe?" His tone purred, like a cat.

There was silence again, until finally the old man said, "Just leave me alone."

"I'll leave you alone, Joe. All you have to do is tell me how to spell your name, that's all, tell me if I've got the right spelling here. That's all I called for, Joe."

"Sure." The old man sounded exhausted.

"Now, here's the spelling I got, Joe, I'll give it to you again. You listen close, and if it's—"

"I heard it the first time," said the weary voice. "You know it's wrong."

"Well, that's what I figured, but I wanted to be sure. Now, how's the right spelling, Joe?"

"Do we have to go through this?"

"Just spell it out for me, Joe. Slow and clear, and I'll write it down here." Younger smiled and picked up his cigar from the ashtray and said, "I've got a pencil right here."

The old man spelled out his alias, slowly, saying each letter as though he were too worn out to hold the phone, as though he'd fall over any minute. He spelled the false name, and when he was done Younger said, "There, now, that wasn't so tough, was it? Why'd you carry on like that, Joe? You get up on the wrong side of the bed this morning?"

"Is that all?"

"For now, Joe."

Younger hung up, and put the cigar between his teeth, and smiled to himself.

6

Younger pulled to a stop in front of the old man's house. He rolled down the windows and turned the two-way radio up to full blast; nothing was coming from it right now but static. Then he got out a fresh cigar, unwrapped it, lit it, and settled down to wait.

After a minute the radio sounded off, a guttural voice, distorted so much by the extra volume that the words couldn't be made out. Younger just sat there while the voice thundered away, and then the voice stopped and there was just the scratching static again.

He didn't look towards the house. He didn't have to. He knew the old man was in there, and he knew the old man could hear that radio, and he knew the old man would have to look out and see him sitting here. Younger didn't have to watch the house to see a curtain rustle, see an old face appear in a window; he knew what would happen, without watching.

Still, nothing happened for a while. Every now and

then the loud voice roared out words that couldn't be understood. Between times the static crackled away, and Younger smoked his cigar down to a stub and threw the stub out the window into the street.

Half an hour went by. Younger didn't move. Nothing happened.

Finally, the screen door on the old man's porch slammed open, crashing around into the wall. Younger turned his head and saw the old man come storming out of the house. He came down the front stoop and along the walk, his knobbly old hands closed up into fists. He came over to the car and bent forward and looked in the window and said, "What are you doing here?"

"Hi, there, Joe. You over your mad?"

"Why are you parked in front of my house?" The old man was trembling all over, hands and head and voice. He looked as though any second he'd leap for Younger's throat.

Younger spread his hands, being innocent. "I'm just taking it easy, Joe," he said. "Out on patrol a while, and then pull to the curb and rest a few minutes."

"You've been out here half an hour!"

"Joe, about that phone call the other day. I've been thinking it over, and if I said anything to offend you, I want you to know I'm sorry."

"You can't keep this up forever, Younger."

"Joe, all I want in this world is for us to be friends. I told you all about my Army experiences because I want you to know about me, just like I want to know about you. Friends, Joe, that's all. Share our experiences."

The old man closed his eyes. He was bent forward, his forearms on the car door, his head framed by the open window. With his eyes closed that way, he almost looked dead; lines of age mingled with lines of weariness and worry in his face, making it look like an overdone pencil sketch.

"Abner Younger and Joe Sheer," Younger said thoughtfully. "It sounds like one of those old-time vaudeville acts, doesn't it? You ever do any vaudeville, Joe?"

The old man's eyes were open again, staring at Younger. "What did you say?"

"I asked you if you ever did any vaudeville."

"What did you call me, you son of a bitch? What name did you say?"

Younger laughed and said, "Oh, come on, Joe, we're pals, you don't have to put on the act for me. I've known your name from the beginning."

The old man shook his head. He acted dazed now. He pushed away from the car, turned and started back for the house, walking as though he were drunk.

Younger let him get halfway to the stoop and then called, "Sheer!" He put steel in his voice now, let all the familiarity and jollity drain out of it. "Come back here!" he shouted, and it was the way a first sergeant shouts it.

Now was the moment of decision. At this point, the

old man had to make up his mind for good and all; he couldn't wait and hope and let things ride any longer. He could choose to try a hopeless bluff, or he could choose to go into the house and lock the doors and break out whatever artillery he had in there for a last-ditch stand, or he could give in completely and come back and turn himself over to Younger for whatever Younger wanted with him.

Nearly a minute went by while the old man stood in front of his house, back to Younger, unmoving, making up his mind. When he finally made his decision, it was the only one he could have made, really, considering everything. He was too smart to try a hopeless bluff, and too old to try a last-ditch stand. He turned around and came back to Younger.

Younger said, "Get in the car." The steel was in his voice to stay; he was in command now, the free ride was over.

The old man got into the car, and sat there wordlessly.

Younger handed him the clipboard and a pen. "In chronological order," he said, "I want you to write down every robbery you were ever in, what year it happened, and how much you got out of it. Not the whole take, just your cut."

Hopeless, the old man whispered, "What do you want from me?"

"I just told you. Now listen close. Do it in three columns, date first and then what city it was and then how much you got. You don't have to worry about the month or anything, just the year."

The old man looked at the pen in his hand and the clipboard on his lap with the blank sheet of paper ready on it. With the same hopelessness in his voice, he said, "I'm not sure I can remember everything."

"You'll remember."

It took nearly half an hour. Younger smoked a cigar and listened to the occasional calls on the radio and watched the little traffic on the street; he felt no impatience. Everything would come, everything in its time. He'd waited fifty-one years, he could wait a little longer.

Finally, the old man said, "There. That's it."

Younger took the list and studied it, and saw nothing listed for Cleveland in 1953. He shook his head and put the list down and smashed the old man backhanded across the face. "Don't lie to me," he said. "Don't ever lie to me again, Sheer." He ripped the top sheet off and handed the clipboard back. "This time," he said, "do it right."

The old man wordlessly started writing again. When he was done this time, there was an entry for Cleveland in 1953. Younger nodded and said, "All right, Sheer, that's good. You can go on now."

The old man looked at him in surprise. "I can what?"

"Get out of the car. Go home."

"For God's sake, Captain Younger, what do you want from me?"

"I'll be back," Younger promised him. "And you'll be here. If you know what's good for you."

7

One million, eight hundred and seventy-six thousand dollars." Younger said it slowly, in rich, round tones, enjoying the sensual feeling of the numbers in his mouth. "You made an awful lot of money, Joe," he said. "An awful lot of money."

They were sitting in the old man's living room, three days after the list had been made up. The old man seemed thinner than before, and more lined, and more hopeless. He was getting ripe, slowly getting ripe, but Younger was in no hurry. When he made the final move, he was going to *know* the old man was ready.

Besides, anticipating was half the pleasure. There was no need to hurry the chase to its conclusion.

"Tell me about it, Joe," he said. He was being affable again today, letting a little slack in the line, not wanting the old man to get so desperate he'd do something stupid, like leave everything behind and run away. He said, "Tell me how these robberies are done. Tell me about, say, the Cleveland robbery, the one in '53."

The old man looked at him. "Why?"

Younger shrugged and smiled and said, "I'm interested, that's all. You're the first man in your job I've ever met. Tell me the whole thing, Joe. First the Cleveland job in '53, and then the Des Moines robbery in '49, and then . . . well, just start."

The old man said, "I don't understand you. I can't figure you out."

"Don't even try, Joe. Just tell me the story of your life."

The old man started, talking hesitantly at first, with long pauses, trying to find the words and trying to understand why he was supposed to talk now. But gradually the tempo speeded up as the old man got into the story, and all the details began to flow: how a robbery was set up, what each man did, what was done in this particular job and that particular job, what went wrong here and what went right there.

From time to time he mentioned a name, and each time, Younger quietly wrote the name down, just to have.

The old man talked, and Younger listened, and slowly the old man was relaxing, was getting interested in the process of telling his stories, treating them like anecdotes, like conversation. Younger was interested, too, enjoying listening as he had earlier on the train enjoyed telling his own anecdotes.

Afternoon lengthened, and the room turned semi-dark, and the old man's voice droned on. Younger smiled and nodded and listened, making his interest obvious. In some strange way it was a good afternoon, one of the best either of them had ever lived.

When it was over, the old man said, "I don't understand you. You're a policeman, you know all this about me, but you don't arrest me. You push me and push me, but then you don't do anything about it. I just can't figure you out, I can't figure out what you want."

Younger, at the door, turned and smiled. "What I want? That's easy. Half. See you soon." He put on his cowboy hat and left.

8

But I don't *have* that much!"

"Sure you do, Joe." Younger was being patient, as patient as a saint. "I showed you the figures, and that's the way it's got to be."

The old man sat there on the sofa, wringing his hands. "You know where all my money is," he said. "It's in banks and mutual funds; it's all invested. I wouldn't have money around in cash like that. Why would I do something as stupid as that?"

"Half a million, Joe," Younger said, enjoying the phrase, liking to say it. "Half a million at least, at the very least. And I want half of it. And my patience is wearing thin, Joe."

"I swear to God, I swear I don't have that much, I don't have anywhere near that much. I swear to God."

Younger sighed and shook his head. "Every one of these sessions I have to wind up slapping you around. I hate to do that, Joe, honest I do. Now let's quit fooling around, for good and all."

"Wait! Wait, please!"

Younger stood over him, hands bunched.

The old man said, "I'll give you what I can, what I have. . . . I have a thousand dollars in the house, I'll give you that. And I'll get the rest of it, everything I have."

"A thousand? Let's see it."

Younger smiled at the old man's back as they went out to the kitchen. A thousand, one measly thousand? It would lead to the rest, at last.

But it didn't. In the kitchen, the old man took a pouch from the flour canister and there was the thousand dollars. But no hint about the rest of it; a half a million couldn't be hidden in flour canisters.

The old man gave him the money, saying, "I'll get you what I can, I'll close out my accounts, sell back my mutual funds—"

"Never mind that stuff, quit talking about that stuff!" Younger slapped the wad of money down on the kitchen shelf, really irritated now. "You think I give a damn about your mutual funds? It's the *cash* I want like this thousand bucks. This is the first thousand, Joe, now where's the rest?"

The old man closed his eyes. He shook his head.

Younger knocked him down.

9

After ringing the bell three times, Younger kicked the door in. He knew the old bastard was in here, so what was he trying to pull? He'd regret this, the old fart, he'd live to regret this.

Except he wouldn't. Younger looked all over the house and finally found the old man hanging from the shower ring in the bathroom, naked and blue, with a face like a gargoyle.

Younger couldn't believe it. Why'd he do it, the miserable bastard? It wasn't as though that was the only way out; he could have handed half his money over to Younger and that would have been an end to it. He could have gone on living, no trouble. Yeah, and *still* have more money left than most men make in a lifetime.

What about the money now? Younger paced around the house, thinking, thinking. Was it gone for good now? His roving eyes searched and searched, trying to *see* the money, trying to look through brick or stone or earth or wood or metal or whatever was hiding the money from view, trying to see it there in stacks and stacks of green, somewhere, somewhere . . .

But where? In the two weeks since the old man had given him the first thousand Younger had gone over this house like a man looking for the other cuff link, and he was just about willing to swear it wasn't here. It wasn't buried in the cellar or the back yard, it wasn't under the floorboards in the attic or behind a false back in a closet or stuffed inside a mattress, it wasn't in the walls or the ceiling or the floor, it wasn't in the furniture or the fixtures, it wasn't anywhere in the house or on the property.

No, and it wasn't in the apartment in Omaha, either. Last week Younger had driven the old man down there and gone through the apartment, and there wasn't anything hidden there at all.

Nor was there any safety deposit box key anywhere in either place. Nor a railroad station locker key. Nor any kind of map. Nor anything else that would even *hint* where the money was.

Sheer didn't have a car. He didn't travel anywhere except to Omaha, and only by train. The area of his life was narrow and prescribed, and Younger knew every inch of it. The money had to be within that area somewhere, and that's all there was to it.

So he'd find it anyway, the old bastard hadn't cheated him after all. Sheer might be dead, but the money was still alive and so was Younger, and sooner or later they'd be getting together.

But first things first. The old man was dead, his body hanging there, and that had to be taken care of before anything else.

It couldn't be called a suicide, he knew that much. Younger hadn't kept his interest in the old man entirely hidden. He'd used patrolmen to help him keep an eye on Sheer, and he'd left Sheer's phone number with the police switchboard as one of the places he might be reached in an emergency. If the old man's death were listed as suicide, with the normal investigation that would follow, this whole business might backfire.

Like the autopsy. If the death was a suicide, there'd be a routine autopsy, and the first thing the doctor would see would be the marks Younger had made on Sheer, the bruises and burns, the cuts and rope marks, the whole history of what Younger had done to try and pry the half million out of the stubborn old bastard's carcass. The doctor would know someone had tortured Sheer, and from there on Younger would be in trouble.

How to make it something other than suicide, though, that was the problem. Younger gnawed at it, pacing back and forth in the living room of the dead man's house, puffing away at a cigar, and finally he remembered Dr. Rayborn.

All that was needed, after all, was a death certificate that didn't say anything about suicide, and Dr. Rayborn should be happy to make one out as a little favor to Captain Younger. Rayborn was another interesting citizen Younger had come across in his first few months on the job; he'd do a favor for Younger, no question. Younger put his cowboy hat on and left the dead man's house and went to see Dr. Rayborn.

Rayborn didn't want to do it, until Younger mentioned Dr. Wash in Omaha, and then Rayborn didn't make any more trouble. Referring a patient to someone else to get an abortion is just as much a felony as doing the abortion yourself.

Gliffe, a little later, was easier to handle. He was in local politics, he wanted to be the county's next coroner, and he was more than happy to do a favor for someone on the inside like Captain Younger, especially after Dr. Rayborn told him they weren't covering a murder but only a suicide. And covering the suicide, Younger added, only to protect the reputations of some innocent parties slandered by the dead man in his suicide note.

It was all smooth and easy. He didn't have to tell either Rayborn or Gliffe a word about the half million. And now it was all his, the whole thing; all he had to do was find it.

The next night he drove out to the dead man's house to start searching again, and a stranger was on the porch, talking to the Ricks boy next door. Younger drove on by, turned around in the next block and followed the stranger back to the Sagamore Hotel, where he was registered as Charles Willis of Miami.

Charles Willis of Miami? What was he doing here, who was he, what did he want with Joe Sheer? One day after Joe dies, this stranger comes in, this big, hard, mean-looking stranger, this Charles Willis of Miami?

He was after the money, that had to be it. A crook, a criminal, one of Joe Sheer's old pals, come to steal the dead man's money.

Maybe this Willis knew where the money was. Maybe all Younger had to do was keep him in sight, and this Willis would lead him right to the cash. Maybe this wasn't so bad, having this Willis here, maybe it was the best break of all.

Younger kept Willis in sight. The next day Willis took the town cab to Lynbrooke and stopped in the newspaper office there. Younger questioned Sammy, the taxi driver, but Sammy didn't know a thing about his passenger.

Younger warned him to keep his mouth shut and not to tell Willis anything about the questions, and then he went on back to his Ford as Willis came out of the newspaper office.

There was something almost frightening about Willis. He was big and rangy and hard-looking, with the coldest eyes Younger had ever seen, and hands as gnarled as tree branches. His clothes fit him like an impatient compromise with society, as though the man inside them could never really be comfortable in a suit and a white shirt, with a tie knotted around his neck and leather shoes encasing his feet.

If it weren't for all the money, Younger might have stayed away from Willis, but half a million dollars was too much to give up, too much. He clung.

But then Willis disappeared, and turned up at
Gliffe's place, and then at Rayborn's. Younger felt
Willis rocking the boat, rocking the boat, and he ran
around town in a panic, trying to find Willis, head him
off, stop him before he blew the whole thing sky high.

Then he did find him, unconscious in the cellar of
the old man's house. Coming down the cellar stairs,
seeing Willis sprawled out there on the floor, Younger
had a terrible urge to kill him, kill him now, as he
might kill a rattlesnake sleeping in the sun. Willis was
defenseless now, and Younger had the opportunity,
and in the holster under his coat he had the method.
He'd never get a second chance, never another chance
like this.

But the money hunger was too strong, and he didn't
do it.

Besides, there was another one now, the man Tiftus,
another stranger slipping into town to get his hands
on Sheer's money. Who knew how many of them
would come in before it was all over, criminals, hard
and dangerous men, brutal men, all after that money?

Then Tiftus was killed, and Younger knew he was in
over his head. He forced a partnership with Willis so
he wouldn't feel so exposed anymore, and then it
turned out Willis didn't know any more about where
the money was than he did.

So they split the job into two halves. Willis would
look for the money, and Younger would look for whoever had killed Tiftus. The killer had to be found;

otherwise, he could be off somewhere getting his hands on the money without anybody knowing about it.

Younger knew he couldn't trust Willis. He knew that Willis, as soon as he found the money, would try to get away with the whole thing. But Younger wasn't that dumb; he had men watching Willis all the time. He would know when Willis got his hands on the money, and a little while later his own hands would be on it.

All of it. Willis would try to double-cross him, wouldn't he? So there was no reason to share, none at all.

10

Younger walked back and forth in the field behind Joe Sheer's house; back and forth, back and forth, his eyes on the weedy, uneven ground. He was looking for the shovel.

The way he had it figured, this was where the shovel would be. Maybe not back here exactly, but somewhere close by, close by. Because the killer *had* hit Willis with the shovel, but he *hadn't* hit Tiftus with it. The state police had finally done something useful; sent him a report on the murder weapon, which wasn't a shovel after all but was a heavy glass ashtray that had already been in the room when the killer got there.

What he couldn't understand was why the killer had taken the shovel away from Joe's place at all. Was he trying to hold up other people from digging down there? That didn't make any sense. And he wouldn't have taken it because of fingerprints either; he could have just wiped it off, like he'd wiped off the ashtray at the hotel.

The only thing Younger could think was that he'd panicked. He'd been crouched behind the cellar door for an hour, in the dark, hearing somebody walk around and not knowing what it was or what he wanted or if he'd open the cellar door, and when it finally did happen and he managed to hit Willis just right, and Willis went crashing on down the stairs, he was probably too rattled to think straight. The farthest thing from his mind was to go downstairs and put the shovel back where he found it. He probably didn't even think about it being in his hand until he was already out of the house.

Well, how far would he go with it? He didn't have it an hour later, when he got to the hotel. So what did he do, go a few steps, a block, two blocks, and then realize he still had the shovel, and throw it away somewhere? That was likeliest.

Except that he maybe had a car. That shovel might right now be on the back seat of a car some place, or in the trunk. If the killer had had a car close by Joe's house, then that's what might have happened.

But Younger was gambling that it wasn't. Younger was gambling the killer had come to Joe's house across the back way here, across the fields, to avoid being seen by anybody, and had gone back the same way, and had most likely thrown the shovel away out here somewhere. That was Younger's theory and he was out here testing it.

Because what he needed was a lead, a starting point, and he didn't have one. He had no idea at all who the killer might be. If his theory that the shovel had been taken out of panic was right, then the killer was an amateur, not a professional like Willis or Tiftus. And if he was an amateur, then he was probably a local citizen.

But who? Nobody knew the whole story here, nobody but Younger. Rayborn and Gliffe each knew their little piece of the story, three of Younger's patrolmen each knew a little piece, but only Younger knew it all. Besides, those five were all clear. He'd checked them, going by where each of them had been during the hour when the killer was hiding in the cellar at Sheer's house and the time when Tiftus was being killed, and all five of them had airtight alibis for at least some part of that time.

Somebody else. Younger wanted to catch a corner of him, just an edge of him, just to get started. And the shovel was it.

Visualize him. Standing behind the cellar door, burlap bag on his head, shovel in his hands. He waits an hour, shaky, scared, then he slugs Willis and runs. He's got to take the burlap bag off his head right away, but that isn't around either. So he's so panicky he runs off with the shovel in one hand and the burlap bag in the other. Out the back door, to be out of sight, and across the fields, and somewhere along the way he drops the shovel and the bag.

Younger could almost see him, see everything but his face, see him running away across the field, crouched over, shovel and burlap bag in his hands.

Then see him pause, stop, look around like a hunted animal, then hurl the shovel and bag away and run on.

Would he think to wipe his fingerprints from the shovel handle? Maybe, but maybe not.

So this was the thing to do: go over the ground himself, every inch of the field back here behind the old man's house. And if the shovel wasn't here, then start questioning the neighbors. Maybe one of them saw the man with the shovel. It was possible, certainly possible, and people would remember something like that, a man running along carrying a shovel.

"Hello, Captain! You looking for something?"

Younger looked up, startled, and there in front of him was a boy of about nineteen, tall, gangly, acned. It took Younger a second to break away from his own thoughts, and then he placed the boy; the Ricks boy, from the house next door to Joe Sheer. The one Willis had been talking to that first night.

Younger said, "Hello, there." What was the boy's first name? Alfred, that was it. "Hello, there, Alfred."

"Maybe I can help," the boy said. "If you lost something."

On the off chance, Younger said, "Did you see a man with a shovel out here yesterday?"

"Man with a shovel?" The boy frowned and shook his head. "I saw a shovel but I didn't see—"

Younger said, "A shovel? Where?"

"Over there, by that red bush. This morning I found it, and a bag, like a potato sack, right next to it."

The captain started off towards the red bush. "Is it still there, do you suppose? If it's still—"

"*I* took them," the boy said. "I didn't think they belonged to anybody, just thrown a—"

"You've got them? Where?"

"In the house, down cellar."

"Show me."

"Sure."

The boy led the way, back to his house and down into the cellar. The shovel and bag were on an old worktable down there.

Younger looked at them and smiled. They'd have the boy's prints all over them now, but there might still be others they could use. At least this proved his theory; the killer had panicked, and run out across the fields carrying the bag and shovel. He was an amateur, probably a local citizen. He could be found.

Younger said, "I'll have to take these along, Alfred. They're evidence, in a case I'm working on. When I'm done, I'll bring them back. Finders keepers. All right?"

The boy shrugged. "You can keep them," he said. "We've got a shovel of our own anyway."

Younger went upstairs and out the front door and headed for his Ford. Before he got there, Willis came out of Joe's house and across the lawn and said, "Where'd you get that stuff?"

Younger was pleased with himself. "I had a theory," he said. "I figured the guy got panicky and—"

"Where'd you get them?"

Irritated, wanting to tell Willis the whole theory, he

said, "The guy threw them away out in the field behind the house."

Willis looked at the Ricks house. "That's where you found them?"

"The kid next door found them."

"Oh."

"What about you?"

Willis shook his head. "No luck so far."

"I don't think the money's in the house. We'd of found it by now."

"I'll keep looking," Willis said. He turned around and went back into the house.

Surly bastard. Younger would be glad to have the partnership done with. He put the shovel and bag in his car and drove away.

PART FOUR

1

Parker went back in the house. He knew Younger would keep himself busy for a while, have fun looking the shovel over for fingerprints. He might even dust the burlap bag.

Inactivity was making Parker irritable, testy. All he did was sit here in Joe Sheer's house and wait for that state cop, Regan, to come up with whoever killed Tiftus. And even then that might not ease the situation. The Willis cover might be loused up no matter what way things went here.

But maybe not. He knew more now than he'd known five minutes ago.

After Younger had driven away with the useless shovel and burlap bag, Parker went over to the side window in the living room and looked over at the house next door. Through the window there he could see another small living room like this one, but more crowded with furniture, and the furniture all older. He looked up, and saw bedroom windows on the second floor, overlooking this window and the window in Joe's kitchen.

The kid was out on the porch again. Parker moved away from the window, across the room and out on the front porch. Only the width of a driveway separated this house from the one next door. Parker called to the kid. "Hey, come over here a minute."

The kid looked at him. "Me?"

"Yeah, come here."

"What do you want?"

"I want to talk to you."

The kid looked around, but there wasn't anyone else in sight. He said, "I got to stay here and listen for the phone."

"This won't take long."

The kid didn't want to do it, but he couldn't come out with a flat refusal and he couldn't think of an excuse. He uhhhhed a few times, and then he said, "All right. But then I gotta get back here and listen for the phone."

"Sure."

The kid came across the lawn and up on the porch. Parker held the door open for him. The kid wouldn't quite meet his eye. He went into the house, and Parker went in after him, shut the door, and said, "Why'd you go to my room in the hotel?"

The kid turned around, wide-eyed and scared. "What? What do you mean?"

Parker shook his head. "Don't waste time. You went

there and Tiftus caught you, and you slugged him. Same as you slugged me when you were in the cellar."

"I don't—I don't know what you're—"

"What I can't figure," Parker told him, "is what you went to my room for. You figure I already had the money?"

"Mister, I swear to you—"

Parker hit him, open-handed. "Don't tell lies," he said. "You're too young."

The kid was going to cry in a second. He put a shaking hand up to where his cheek was turning red, and he said, "I don't know why you—"

"You're a watcher," Parker told him. "I've seen you on the porch, I've seen you at the window in the living room. You stand and watch."

"There's nothing wrong with that. What's wrong with that?"

Parker said, "Younger was putting pressure on Joe, on the old guy that lived here. You watched. Sometimes, at night, you snuck over by a window here and listened."

The kid was shaking his head. His mouth was open, his eyes were wide open.

Parker said, "You believed that crap about the half million dollars. You're as dumb as Younger."

"Cr-crap?"

"It doesn't exist. Joe didn't have any cash buried anywhere. All his dough was invested, just like he told Younger."

"B-but he, he did all those—" The kid stopped

abruptly, and put his other hand up to his face, too. Both hands covered the lower half of his face, and above them he stared at Parker.

Parker nodded. "He did all those robberies. And spent it. Spent it faster than you or Younger could dream."

"I didn't—"

"You did. You were down there digging. You heard me come in, and you waited, and you clubbed me when I opened the cellar door, and you ran back home and hid in a closet. You were so scared you forgot to drop the shovel, that's why you had it to give to Younger. Afraid to hold on to it, so you told him you found it. Younger's dumb, but he'll catch on after a while."

"I didn't do it." The kid shook his head back and forth, back and forth. "I didn't do it. I listened, I heard what they were saying, but I didn't do any of that, I swear it."

Parker said, "There's just one thing I want to know. Why you went to my room in the hotel. I can't figure it."

"No, I didn't do any of that, I didn't—"

Parker slapped him twice, forehand and backhand. The kid blubbered, and Parker said, "I want to know. I don't like things I can't figure."

The kid wailed, "You'll tell the police! You'll turn me in to the police!"

"No. I don't talk to the law."

The kid blinked, and blinked, and stared at Parker. "Do you mean that? Do you mean it?"

"I worked with Joe, in the old days. I don't talk to the law."

The kid rubbed his eyes with a trembling hand, and licked his dry lips. "I didn't mean to do any of it," he said. "Hit you, or that other man, or any of it. I just wanted the money."

"Why'd you go to my hotel room?"

"I wanted to know who you were. I forgot to look in your wallet when I knocked you out, and I was afraid to come back, because maybe you weren't still unconscious. I figured I had to know who you were, because of you searching the house and all. I didn't know, maybe you were with the FBI or something."

"How'd you find my room?"

"I was following Captain Younger, and he was following you. Before that, before I hit you."

"So you went in and Tiftus caught you there."

"He came in the window. I hid, behind the dresser, but he saw me. He started to holler and run, and I was scared, and I hit him with the ashtray. I didn't know that could kill him, honest. I just wanted to knock him out, I didn't know it could kill him."

All along Tiftus had thought Parker knew more about Joe's goods than he did. The inside track, he'd said one time; Parker had known Joe well and so had the inside track. Tiftus must have thought there might be a letter from Joe or something like that, something to give Parker that inside track, and he'd gone looking for it.

The kid was shivering, like he'd just been doused with cold water. He said, "You won't tell the police, will you? Will you?"

The kid was trouble. He knew everything, he'd heard everything that Joe had told Younger. And he'd be grabbed; sooner or later he'd be grabbed. He'd done one moronic thing after another, even to giving Younger the shovel and burlap bag. Sooner or later Younger or Regan, more likely Regan, would get to the kid, and the kid would do nothing but talk. He'd talk three days straight, and not repeat himself once.

Parker shook his head. Another item to cover. He said, "There's nobody home at your place?"

"No. My mother's out—"

"All right. You got to clear out of town for a while. I'll give you some money."

"You will?" The kid lit up with hope.

"Write a note, so your mother doesn't get the law looking for you."

"Oh. Sure. That's easy."

"We'll do that first."

Parker took him to the kitchen and found pencil and paper, and the kid wrote the note. Parker read it. It would do. He said, "Move fast. Go next door, pack a few things, not much. Then come back here."

"Yes, sir."

The ten minutes the kid was gone were bad. Parker

paced back and forth, back and forth. Too many things could go wrong.

But the kid came back, carrying a small satchel. "I'm packed," he said. "I left the note on the dining-room table."

"Good," Parker said, and hit him twice.

He buried him in the cellar in the hole the kid had dug himself.

2

Parker went out the back way. He knew Younger had men on stakeout, to see he didn't try to clear out of town, but he didn't figure Younger's troops to be any brighter than their leader. He'd long since marked the grey Plymouth parked down the block that was used by the man watching the front of the house, and the green Dodge parked beside the road across the fields would be the guy watching the back. If there'd been a third station he'd have found it by now, so all he had to do was go between the Plymouth and the Dodge.

He went the back-yard route, keeping close to the houses, and went a block and a half before coming out onto the street. Then he walked directly downtown.

He got into the hotel the same way he'd come out the first time; the fire escape around back. He remembered Tiftus' room number and knew the woman Rhonda would be in the room next door.

She opened the door right away when he knocked. "It's you," she said. "It's about time."

He stepped in and shut the door. She was wearing black stretch pants and a pink sweater and she was completely made up. He said, "Where were you going?"

"Nowhere. You told me to come here and stay put, I come here and stay put. I was beginning to think you forgot me."

She was being cute. She must figure he was here for sex. He said, "We both want out of this town, right?"

She nodded, and then shrugged her shoulders. "It ain't the sort of place I'm used to, let's put it that way."

"We can't go until the law gets whoever did for Tiftus, right?"

"That's me, baby," she said. "Not you. You're in the clear, remember? Your buddy cop give you an alibi."

"It's straight," he said. "I wouldn't kill Tiftus, I got no reason. Killing him just loused things."

"Boy, I'll say. And let me tell you something, I liked that guy. He was little, and he had a kind of a funny name, but I liked him. He appreciated me, that's why."

"Sure."

"He told me some things about you," she said. "What he told me, it didn't seem like you'd be the guy killed him. I mean, even if you were going to, you know? You'd have more sense than do it right in your own room like that."

"Fine." He had to let her ramble a minute; if he tried to hurry her, she'd just get her back up.

She said, "So I don't see why you got to stick around. *I* got to, because that cop, that Regan, he told me to. But you're in the clear."

"Not all the way," he said. "Not till Regan's satisfied."

"Listen," she said, "who's in charge around here, anyway? Is it Regan, or is it your buddy, the fat one?"

"Younger's in charge, but Regan's the cop."

"Well, that's just dandy. Are they ever gonna get the guy that did it?"

"No."

She hadn't expected that answer. She shook her head and said, "What? Why the hell not?"

"Because I got him," Parker told her. "It's a long story, you don't want to hear it."

"Are you kidding? Sure I want to hear it."

"You don't."

She looked at his face, and for a second or two she was going to argue, and then she changed her mind. "Okay, I don't," she said. "So what's the point?"

"The point is, we've got to give Regan somebody else."

"Like who, for instance?"

"Anybody. Somebody not here anymore."

"And he's supposed to swallow it?"

"Younger is, and he will. It's got to be just a good enough story so Younger can get away with accepting it and closing the case. Once Younger calls the case solved, there's nothing Regan can do anymore. He's only in like on an advisory capacity, till they find out who did it."

Doubtfully she said, "All right, if you say so. How do we tell this story?"

"It depends. What did you tell Regan so far?"

"Hah. Which time? He wouldn't trust me across the street, that Regan. First I tell him one thing, then I tell him something else."

Impatience was getting to Parker. Younger might take it into his head to drop by Joe's house any time, and Parker didn't want Younger upset. He wanted Younger thinking he had everything under control.

He said, "Just tell me what you told him."

She shrugged and waved her arms and said, "The first time, I told him the truth. The second time, I told him I made a mistake." She walked across the room and got herself a cigarette from the dresser.

"Get me one, too," he said. This was going to take a while.

She smoked a filter brand. She gave him one and he ripped the filter off it before he took a light from the match she held up for him. She looked at him with brown eyes, steadily, while he lit his cigarette. She still thought he was there for sex.

He wasn't. Maybe later, when this was all cleared up. He still had one woman waiting for him in Miami, but he'd been getting tired of her anyway. Later on he'd make up his mind, not now.

He sat down in the leatherette chair and said, "Tell

me what you told him the first time. Detail by detail. Tell me like I'm him and you're doing it just like you did."

"I don't see the point, but why not?" She sat down in the other chair, crossed her legs, and looked up at the ceiling. "Dear Inspector Regan," she said, "it all began when I was five years . . ."

"I don't have time for that, Rhonda."

Something in his voice drained the cuteness out of her. "All right," she said, flat. "This is what I told him. Adolph and I come here on vacation, just passing through. Adolph saw you in the lobby when we came in, and said he knew you and he was going to go say hello. I don't know what went on between you, but you beat him up and threatened to kill him. That's it."

"What about bringing him back to his room? What about running into you there?"

She shook her head. "No. I didn't say anything about that, I just did it straight and simple. You beat him up and he came back to the room afterwards and told me you were the one did it."

"You told Regan that? That Tiftus came back to the room afterwards and told you I beat him up?"

"Yes."

"How did you say Tiftus said it? Did you say he used my name, or said it was the guy he'd seen in the lobby that beat him up, or what?"

Details seemed to bother her. She was getting irritated, and now she shrugged her shoulders, blew cigarette smoke, and said, "How do I know? I didn't give the cop a play by play."

"All right, listen. This is what you told Regan: You and Tiftus came here, saw a guy in the lobby that Tiftus said he knew, Tiftus went away to see the guy and came back and said the guy beat him up. Right?"

She nodded. "Just what I said."

"All right. So what did you tell him the second time?"

"That you weren't the guy. When I first saw you in that office there, I figured you'd done it, and I did like that guy whether you believe it or not, so that's why I fingered you like I did. But then I got to thinking, and you come up with the alibi and the buddy-buddy with the cop, so when I saw Regan again I told him I made a mistake, you weren't the guy after all."

"You told him I wasn't the guy Tiftus saw in the lobby."

"Right."

Parker thought it over. He'd already told Regan that Tiftus had gone to see him that morning, and that he'd seen Tiftus on the street a while later. He had to include that, plus what the woman had already told Regan, and make it all work out to a story that pointed off in some brand new direction.

While he thought, she just sat there in the other chair, smoked her cigarette, and watched him. She seemed a little puzzled, and hesitated.

After a while he said, "All right, we got a new story to tell Regan. We don't change the old story, we just add to it. You and Tiftus got here, saw a guy in the lobby, Tiftus said he knew him, went away, came back, and said the guy beat him up and threatened to kill him. When you saw me you thought I was the guy, but you were wrong. The guy was tall and built like me, but younger, and he had blond hair. And what you remember is, Tiftus told you his name. When he saw the guy in the lobby he said, 'Why, there's Jimmy Chambers.' You got that? He said, 'Why, there's Jimmy Chambers.' "

She nodded. "Why, there's Jimmy Chambers," she said. "But I don't get the point."

"Don't worry about it. I'll get something else going on Jimmy Chambers from the other side, through Younger."

"But who is this Jimmy Chambers? Is that just a name you made up?"

"No. It's a guy with a record, Regan won't have any trouble finding out there's a real Jimmy Chambers, and Jimmy Chambers did know Tiftus, so everything's going to check."

She said, "He wasn't really in town, was he?"

"No. Now, after . . ."

She said, "I can't do that."

"You can't do what?"

"I can't get this fella Chambers in trouble. Why don't we just make up some name, it'd be the same."

"No, it wouldn't. Chambers is a name Regan can check. And Chambers got killed in an explosion a few

months ago and nobody official knows about it, so
don't worry about getting him in trouble."

"Is that the truth?"

"Happened on a job we were both on. I don't sic
the law on my own kind."

"All right," she said. "When do you want me to do
this?"

"Tomorrow morning."

"They're burying him tomorrow morning."

He had to think for a second, and then he realized
she meant Tiftus. He said, "Then Regan will be with
you at the funeral. Tell him then."

"It just occurs to me, like that?"

"No. You remembered it tonight, and you weren't
going to say anything because you didn't think Regan
trusted you. But you want to see your man avenged, so
you're going to tell him anyway."

"I hope he'll believe me," she said.

"Don't worry about it."

"Sure." But then she brightened and said, "I can do
a real scene, a whole graveside bit. Cry and carry on
and throw myself on the coffin, the whole thing. I
never done anything like that before."

He said, "Don't overdo it, that's all."

"Don't you worry about me," she told him. "You
may not have realized it, but I am by profession an
actress."

"Good." He got to his feet in a hurry to be gone.

She said, "You got to go already? Stick around
awhile."

"Some other time."

She gave him an actress smile. "You want a rain check?"

"Yeah."

3

It was nearly midnight before Younger called back. Parker had been sitting in the dark in the living room of Joe's house, waiting. He'd come back from seeing Rhonda a little before ten, and called police headquarters to leave a message for Younger to call him. Then two hours went by, and Parker just sat and waited, not thinking about anything in particular, not planning, not being impatient or irritable. It worked that way with him sometimes, when he knew where he stood and how the play should go from there on; he could sit alone in the dark and wait, as silent and patient as a stone.

Until finally the phone rang and it was Younger. The first thing he said was, "You found it?"

"No. I want to talk to you."

"What about?"

"The money, and something else. Come on over here."

"It's late, Willis."

"We've got to get this done tonight. You're going to Tiftus' funeral tomorrow?"

"Regan wants me to go. Him, too, he's coming along."

"Good. Come over here now, it won't take long."

Younger grumbled, but after a while he said he'd be right there. Parker hung up and got to his feet and went around the house turning on lights. He knew other people thought it strange when he sat in the dark, and he didn't want Younger geechy about anything. He made himself a cup of coffee and went back to the living room to wait, and ten minutes later the doorbell rang.

When Parker opened the door, Younger came in complaining. "You know it's after midnight? This better be worth it."

"Sit down, Younger, this won't take long."

They both sat down in the living room, and Parker said, "I want you to think about something. You're looking for the guy killed Tiftus. But Regan's looking for him, too. What if Regan comes up with him first?"

"I take him right away from him. I'm still in charge, Willis, I already told you that."

Parker shook his head. "No. You take him away after Regan tells you he's got him. Is Regan going to tell you right away?"

"He sure as hell better." Younger was insulted at the idea.

"Why?" Parker asked him. "What if he holds the guy

an hour, six hours, questions him a little, and doesn't say anything to you till he's done with the guy. What do you do about it?"

"I could put in a complaint against him, God damn it!"

"What would that mean to Regan? What would it mean to his bosses? Some hick little town police chief teed off because Regan didn't hold his hand and keep calling him on the phone."

It was true, and Younger had to know it. He tried to bluster, but it didn't work. He said, finally, "What's the point? What difference does it make?"

"If Regan gets him first," Parker told him, "Regan will make him spill. You know he will. He thinks there's something going between you and me anyway. He's suspicious. He won't turn the guy over to you until he finds out what's going on, and then it's too late, the whole thing's out in the open, and we don't stand a chance to get the money."

Younger took out a cigar and fooled with it in his hands but didn't unwrap or open it. He said, "So what can we do?"

"Get the case closed. Turn up a killer, so it gets Regan out of the picture."

"How do we do that? You mean frame somebody? We couldn't get away with it, not even me, I couldn't get away with it."

"We don't have to have a body," Parker told him, "just a name. What you got to do, you got to go straight down to headquarters and send off a teletype request to Washington, you want any information on a man named Jimmy Chambers, known to be an associate of a man named Adolph Tiftus."

"Jimmy Chambers? What the hell for?"

"Shut up and listen to me." Younger looked insulted again, but he didn't say any more, and Parker went right on, not noticing any looks Younger gave him. "Today, this afternoon, I told you something I'd been holding back. I told you something Tiftus said to me when I saw him in the street before he got killed. Remember my story with Regan? I saw Tiftus twice, the first time when he came to my hotel room and a little while later on the street."

Younger nodded. "I remember."

"All right. What he said to me when I met him on the street, I saw he'd been in a fight and he said to me, 'Jimmy Chambers roughed me up.' I said to him, 'I didn't know he was in town,' and he said, 'I guess he came here for the funeral.' That's all. You got it?"

Younger repeated the dialogue, and said, "What's the point? Who the hell is this Chambers?"

"You'll get the answer tomorrow from Washington."

"Then what happens?"

"Then you decide Chambers killed Tiftus, and you thank Regan for helping, and you send him home."

"Just on your say-so?"

"No. There'll be more evidence, don't worry about it."

"What evidence?"

"Wait for it. You want to be able to act surprised when you get it. The important thing is, you send that request out tonight, as quick as you can get downtown, and you tell Regan about it first thing tomorrow morning. You got that? The first thing you see Regan tomorrow morning, you tell him about Chambers. It's important you do it right away."

"All right, all right. Is that all?"

"Yeah. Then, with Regan out of the way, we can look for the money and the killer ourselves."

"Yeah," said Younger, "what about the money? I'm getting closer to the killer all the time, I found the shovel and everything, but what about you? You're just sitting here."

"I've gone through this place," Parker told him. "Tomorrow afternoon, after Regan's out of the case, I think we better go down to Omaha, take a look at Joe's apartment there."

"I've already been through that apartment, Willis. If the money was there, I would have found it."

Parker shook his head. "I want to look at the place myself. You want me to go alone?"

"Not on your life," Younger told him.

Parker shrugged. "Then we'll go together. We'll go in your car, that'll be best. Pick me up here around three o'clock."

"You think Regan will be out of the case by then?"

"Why not? You put a rush on the request to Washington, you get an answer tomorrow morning, Regan is out by noon."

"If he's out," Younger said, "I'll come by. If he isn't I won't. That's the best I can say."

"That's good enough. Get downtown now and send that request off. You can tell Regan you sent it off this afternoon."

"Sure, I already got that."

Parker let him out, waited five minutes, and then went out the back door and down behind the houses again. He was going to need a gun tomorrow, and now was the time to get it.

Downtown was silent and deserted. Electric clocks were aglow deep within the stores along the main street, a few red neon signs here and there were left on all night, and the railroad station and hotel made a little island of light in the middle of it all, but there was no traffic on the street, there were no pedestrians on the sidewalks.

Parker found a sporting goods store on a side street, half a block from the main drag. A rear window was butter under his hands, and he prowled through the fourth-rate stock, mostly rifles and scopes, and finally picked out a pistol for himself, a snub-nose Iver Johnson Trailsman .22. He grabbed a box of ammunition and went back out the window again, adjusting things behind himself to cut down the chances of the theft being noticed right away.

He went back to Joe's house, sat at the kitchen table, and took the gun apart. After he cleaned the oil off it he put it back together again and loaded it. He slept with it under his pillow.

4

It was Regan at the door. Parker said, "Come in."

Regan looked curious and displeased. He nodded, stepped into the house, and said, "I wanted to talk to you."

"Sure." Parker shut the door. "Official business?"

Regan made a disgusted mouth. "Unofficial," he said. "I'm not connected with the Tiftus killing anymore."

"I didn't know that. Come in and sit down."

Regan moved on into the living room, but he didn't sit down. He was wearing a cheap topcoat, and his hands were in the pockets. With his grey crewcut and eyeglasses and hard mouth and the topcoat he didn't look like a college teacher anymore, he looked like what he was; a hard, smart cop, smelling something wrong and not wanting to let go.

Parker stayed on his feet, too. He said, "You found out who killed Tiftus?"

Regan said, "You'd know more about that than I

would." He glanced around the room. "I wish I'd met Joseph Shardin," he said. "He's the key to this whole thing."

Parker said, "Why would I know about it?"

"You were the one solved it," Regan told him. He was being sarcastic, but quietly, not pushing it. "You gave us the clue we needed."

"You mean about Jimmy Chambers?"

"That's who."

"He did it, then, huh?"

"It looks that way. Abner's convinced."

"But you're not."

Regan shook his head. "No, Willis, I'm not. It doesn't make any difference; I'm not in charge."

"You want to ask me something," Parker told him, "go right ahead. I mean to co-operate."

"Why?"

"Because I don't want you down on Charles Willis."

Regan frowned studying him. "I even think that's the truth," he said. "And I don't get it. Why'd you wait so long to tell about Chambers?"

"At first, I figured he couldn't of done it. Then, nobody else turned up that might of, so it had to be him. I figured to begin with if I told about him, you and Younger would grab him and not look anywhere else, because he's served time. But if he really did do the job, I won't want to cover for him. Did you get him yet?"

Regan shook his head. "He doesn't seem to be around town anymore."

"Well, that figures, if he did it."

"Everything figures," Regan said. "A little late, but it all figures. All the different stories that didn't connect so good before, all of a sudden they all go together like magnets. There's some link-up between you and Abner and the Samuels woman, and I can't find it."

"I didn't know either of those two before this all happened," Parker said.

"I believe that, too," Regan told him. "That's why I can't figure it out." He walked around the living room, looking at the furniture. "Shardin's the key," he said, more to himself than Parker. "He dies, and three old friends come to the funeral, a businessman from Miami and two ex-cons. One of the ex-cons kills the other, and the businessman is all of a sudden buddy-buddy with the local captain of police. And with the girlfriend of the murdered man, let's not forget that. First she identifies him as the guy who killed her man, and then she changes her story, and then she changes it again to this Chambers right around the same time the businessman comes up with Chambers. That's a funny thing, isn't it, Willis? I never heard a word about this man Chambers until this morning, and then I hear it from everywhere."

"I told Younger yesterday. What about the woman, what did she say?"

Regan gave a sour smile. "That's right, you weren't there, you wouldn't know. This morning she remembered, Tiftus told her the name of the man who beat him up, and it was Chambers."

"That's what he told me, too."

Regan looked at Parker, and then some more at the room. "I'd like to know how Shardin died," he said.

"I heard it was a heart attack."

"I heard the same thing. All right, Willis, I just wanted to know why you took so long to tell us about Chambers, and you had an answer right on tap."

"It's the truth."

"I'm sure of it." Regan shrugged, and turned towards the door. "It's not my worry anymore," he said. "Chambers'll be found sooner or later, and maybe some more will come out at the trial. I can't wait."

"Fine," said Parker.

Regan walked across the living room to the foyer. "It's been interesting knowing you, Willis," he said.

There was nothing to say to that. Parker held the door open. Regan paused in the doorway and said, "I suppose you'll be leaving town now."

"Probably."

"Well. Good-bye, Willis."

"Good-bye."

5

Younger arrived at three o'clock on the button. Parker didn't wait for him to get out of his Ford and come ring the bell; as soon as he saw Younger pull to a stop at the curb he picked up his suitcase and walked out of the house.

When he opened the car door Younger said, "How come the suitcase?"

"We may have to stay over. We're getting a late start."

"You should have told me, I'd've packed a bag of my own."

Parker didn't want that. He said, "You can borrow from me. No problem." He tossed the suitcase onto the back seat and slid in beside Younger in front. He pulled the door shut and said, "Let's get out of here."

"Right."

Parker nodded at the Plymouth parked down the block. "You want to wake your boy on the way by?"

"What?"

"He's been asleep most of the time the last couple of days. He must have found something steady for the nights."

Younger frowned and said, "How long did you know about him?"

"From the time he parked there."

"Son of a bitch." Younger yanked at the steering wheel, started the Ford away from the curb, and they did a tight U-turn and rode away from the house and the Plymouth both. Younger said, "If you know about him, and if he was always asleep, how come you stuck around?"

"The money," Parker told him. It was an answer Younger could understand.

Younger did. He turned and gave Parker a fat grin. "You want it as bad as I do," he said. "As bad as I do."

"Sure."

"I know it." Younger faced front again, watching the traffic. He was pleased with himself. He said, "Everything went fine with Regan. That was good, when the Samuels woman started talking about Chambers, too. You worked that real well."

"She did it right, huh?"

"Listen, I almost believed her myself. A regular actress. The only thing, what happens when Chambers is picked up?"

"He won't be," Parker told him.

"You sound sure of it."

"I am."

They didn't do any more talking for a while. Younger

took them on a route that didn't go through downtown and that was good. There was less chance of anyone noticing the two of them together in the car. Not that it made that much difference.

After a while, out on the three-lane road that led to Omaha, Younger started again, saying, "You're from Miami, huh?"

"I live there sometimes."

"That's what I'm gonna do. Once I get my hands on that money, I'm clearing out of here. What do you think, Miami? Or would I do better out of the country, maybe go to the Riviera, or Acapulco?"

"One place is like another," Parker told him, but he knew Younger wouldn't be able to understand it.

He didn't. "Not with half a million dollars," he said.

"A quarter of a million," Parker reminded him.

Younger reacted like a kid caught playing hooky; guilty smile and all. "That's right," he said. "That's right, you're right, Willis. I meant to say quarter of a million, that's what I meant."

"Sure."

"You can trust me."

"No. I can't trust you, you know that. And you can't trust me. You don't trust me, that's why you had the guys in the Plymouth and the Dodge."

"You knew about them both?"

"We don't trust each other," Parker told him. "We can't, there's too much money in it. And that isn't any good. Watching each other all the time, we'll never get anywhere. The guy that killed Tiftus is still around some place, remember."

"I'm getting close to him, Willis."

"That isn't the point."

Younger nodded, facing straight ahead as he drove. "I know that. You're right, we got to be able to trust each other."

"That's what I say."

"But how?" Younger turned his head and glanced at Parker, and then faced front again. "I'll tell you the truth, Willis, you could swear on a stack of Bibles the sun was shining and I'd have to go out and look for myself. There's no way on earth you could make me trust you."

"There's one way."

"How?"

"I let you get something on me, so if I double-cross you it backfires."

Younger squinted at the road, trying to figure it out. "I don't get what you mean," he said.

Parker told him, "I write a note. I say, 'I killed Adolph Tiftus.' I sign my name to it. It's all in my handwriting, so you've got me cold. I give you the note, and you give it to a lawyer or a friend or somebody for safekeeping. You tell him, if anything happens to you they should give the note to the law. That way, you're safe. I don't dare touch you."

Younger nodded. "That makes sense," he said. "That isn't a bad idea at all. I could trust you after that."

"Sure."

"We'll do it, then," he said. "As soon as we get back to town."

"We can do it in Omaha, at Joe's apartment. The sooner we do it, the better for both of us."

Younger shrugged. "Okay, fine. I don't care. Only thing, what about me giving you an alibi?"

"I'll cover it in the note. Say I told you it was earlier than it was, and you didn't have a watch on you, something like that. The whole thing'll be worked out in the note."

"Good. That's a good idea."

"For you, too," Parker told him.

Younger looked startled. He glanced at Parker, and away. "What do you mean, me, too?"

"You write a note, too."

"What? That I killed Tiftus? It wouldn't make any sense."

"No, that you killed Joseph Shardin."

Younger now looked scared. "I didn't kill him! What the hell are you talking about, Willis, I didn't kill him!"

"I didn't kill Tiftus," Parker reminded him. "That isn't the point. The point is to have something on you, like you'll have on me."

"But it don't make any sense. How's it gonna look?"

Parker said, "You write, 'I killed Joseph Shardin. I was trying to extort money from him, and I didn't mean to kill him.' And you sign your name. No, wait a second.

Besides that, you write, 'Doctor Rayborn knows all
about it.' Because he does, doesn't he?"

Young glowered at the road. "If that bastard's been
opening his mouth—"

"He didn't have to. I haven't seen him since he fixed
up my face."

"I don't like it," Younger said. "I didn't kill the old
man, why should I say I did?"

Parker told him, "You'll have my note about killing
Tiftus, I'll have your note about killing Joe. That way,
we're safe from each other."

Younger gnawed on his lower lip, and shook his
head back and forth. "I don't like it," he said. "I just
don't like it."

Parker sat back in the seat and watched the flat
countryside roll by. Flat farmland, not a tree in sight.
You could see white farmhouses miles away across the
flat fields.

Sitting at the wheel, driving down the straight road,
Younger chewed his lip and tried to get used to having
only a quarter of a million dollars. That was the problem, and Parker knew it. Younger had been counting
on the whole pie, and now he was having to shift his
thinking, having to gear down to half a pie.

Half a pie in the sky.

With the outskirts of Omaha lumping up ahead of
them, Younger finally nodded. "All right," he said. "It's
the best way."

Parker knew what he meant. He meant he wasn't

that sure anyway that he could get Parker before Parker got him.

"You're right," Parker told him.

6

Parker's note read:

> I killed Adolph Tiftus. He came in my room and we ar-
> gued and I hit him with the ashtray. Then I went to Joe
> Shardin's house and saw Captain Younger and told him it
> was half an hour earlier than it was. I scared Rhonda
> Samuels into making up the story about Jim Chambers.
>
> Charles Willis

Younger read it and said, "Fine. That covers the
whole thing."

They were sitting at the kitchen table in Joe
Sheer's Omaha apartment. Parker had found pen
and paper and had written his note first, to keep
Younger from getting suspicious. Now he pushed the
pen and the pad of paper across the desk and said,
"Your turn."

"Sure," said Younger, but he kept holding Parker's
note, and there was a thoughtful look in his eye.

Parker told him, "Forget it. You still need me. You need me to find the dough, and you need me to help you when you find the guy that killed Tiftus."

"I didn't have any plans," Younger said. He put the note down, took the pen, and started to write. Parker watched him and waited.

This was a quiet neighborhood Joe had picked. There wasn't a sound coming in the kitchen window, not a sound anywhere but the ballpoint pen sliding over the paper as Younger wrote his suicide note.

When it was done, Parker took it and read it:

> I killed Joseph Shardin. I didn't mean to, I was trying to extort money from him and it was an accident. Dr. Rayborn knows all about it, he helped me cover it up. He had to, because I had something on him.
>
> Capt. Abner L. Younger

Younger said, "How is it?"

"Fine," said Parker, and took the .22 pistol out of his pocket. "Keep your palms flat on the table," he said.

Younger's eyes got bigger. He said, "What are you gonna do?"

Parker reached out for the note he'd written, crumpled it, and stuffed it in his pocket. Then he got to his feet. "You don't move," he said. "You don't make a single move."

"You found it," Younger said. His voice was bitter and disgusted. "You found it. It was in the house there all the time."

"I didn't find a dollar," Parker told him. "Joe told you the truth, there wasn't any half million."

"You're lying."

Parker shook his head. "No more," he said. "There's no more reason to lie."

Younger raised his eyes and looked at Parker's face and saw what Parker meant. He said, "You can't do this. You can't get away with it."

Carefully, so he wouldn't wrinkle it, Parker picked up Younger's note and put it up on top of the refrigerator, where it would be out of Younger's reach.

Younger said, "If there isn't any money, you don't have to kill me."

"I can't trust you," Parker told him. "I can't ever trust you. If I let you live, you'll always think the half million's around somewhere; you'll think I've got it."

"No. No, I won't, I'll—"

"We'll talk about it," Parker promised. "But first I want your gun. I don't want you armed while we talk about it."

"We can talk about it," Younger said nodding. "You're right, we can talk about it. There's always some other way to do things, you don't have to—"

"Your gun," Parker said. "Reach in under your coat and take it out and put it on the table. When you take it out, just use your thumb and first finger and just hold it by the butt. And move slow and careful."

"Sure thing, Willis. I won't try anything." Younger was sweating now, scared and eager, trying to find some reason to think he might be alive fifteen minutes from now. He took his pistol out the way Parker had told him, and put it down on the table.

It was a .32, a Smith & Wesson Model 30. Parker took a clean white handkerchief from his pocket and picked Younger's pistol up in his right hand. He held the .22 now in his left.

Younger's hands were still pressed palm down on the Formica table-top, but they were trembling anyway. He watched Parker, and he kept smiling. He was smiling with nerves, and with some stupid idea that a smile would show Parker he was really an all-right guy after all, and with fear. He said, "I believe you, Willis. There isn't any money. I believe you."

"Too late," Parker told him. He walked around the table and stuck the .32 up close against Younger's chest, at an angle the way it would be if Younger were holding the gun himself in his right hand. Younger's mouth opened, and his hands started to come up from the table to protect himself, and Parker pulled the trigger.

After that, it took less than five minutes to get everything arranged. He closed Younger's hand around the .32, he put the note back down on the table and wiped it with the cloth where he'd handled one corner, and he removed his prints from the few things he'd touched in the room. From then on, anything he touched he held with the handkerchief. He went through the apartment the way he'd gone through Joe's house, making sure there was nothing in here to lead to him or anyone else Joe knew from the old days. He got the envelope from Younger's pocket with the list of Joe's jobs and the names, and he burned it in an ashtray along with the note he'd written about killing Tiftus. He flushed the ashes down the toilet.

When he was done, everything was satisfactory. This should answer Regan's questions. Regan had wanted to know about Joseph Shardin, so here it was. Younger had been extorting the old man, and accidentally killed him. Three of Shardin's old friends had come to town for the funeral, one of them had killed the second, and the third didn't have anything to do with it. The third had maybe suspected what Younger had done to the old man, but he hadn't been able to prove anything so he hadn't said anything. When the investigation into the killing of Tiftus was done, this third man left. Younger, feeling remorse, went into Omaha to the old man's apartment there—proving he'd had the run of the old man's life and goods—and there he wrote a suicide note and killed himself.

Fine. The only thing left to do was to get Rhonda Samuels out of town. If she were left there she might get sore and start blowing whistles.

Parker took one last look around and saw that everything was done here. He left the apartment.

1

Parker went into one of the phone booths in the row and copied down the number. Then he walked across the terminal to the Western Union office on the other side. A loud metallic voice was calling out train departures.

In the Western Union office, Parker took a blank and made out a telegram to Rhonda Samuels, Sagamore Hotel, Sagamore, Nebraska. He gave her the number of the phone in the booth across the way and wrote: "Call me six o'clock from pay phone." He handed this across the desk to the woman, who said, "You forgot to sign it, sir."

"No name," Parker told her. "They'll know who it's from."

"It has to have a name," she said.

He leaned towards her, making the effort to be patient and friendly, and winked. "It's a kind of gag," he said.

"Oh." She smiled. "Very well."

He paid for the telegram, and then went out and across the terminal to the restaurant. He had a meal that was too late to be called lunch, too early to be called dinner. He sat awhile over his second cup of coffee, and then went out and wandered around the terminal awhile. At ten minutes to six he went and sat on the little stool in the phone booth.

She didn't call till five after the hour. Parker picked the receiver up on the first ring, and put it to his ear, but he didn't say anything. There was silence a few seconds, and then a voice said, hesitantly, "Hello?"

He recognized her. He said, "Yeah, it's me."

"Oh," she said. "There you are."

"You ready to leave that town?"

"No kidding."

"Buy two tickets on the train to Omaha. Be sure you buy two."

"And you'll reimburse me, won't you?"

"Don't worry about it. Take the next train down here. One leaves there at six-twenty, it gets here quarter to seven."

"I'm not even packed yet."

"So pack. Remember, buy two tickets."

"I remember."

He hung up, and left the phone booth, and waited. At twenty to seven he got his suitcase from the locker where he'd stashed it, and at quarter to she came up the ramp from the tracks and he fell in beside her.

She said, "Don't tell me, let me guess. We came in together, right?"

"Right."

"Together all the way, right?"

"Right."

"So now what? Miami?"

"Tomorrow."

"What about tonight?"

"I got us a hotel room."

"Another hotel room," she said.

"This one's different," he said. He took her arm.

8

There were things Parker couldn't know, things that made the whole structure break apart.

The suicide note. It was a fine suicide note, except it wasn't accurate. When the law went to Dr. Rayborn, he denied everything for a while, and when he finally did break down he said that what he'd helped Younger cover up was a suicide, not a murder. Joseph Shardin had hanged himself, Rayborn said, and he wouldn't change the story.

Regan was running the investigation this time, the whole thing was his, and he wasn't about to let go. It took time, but he got a court order to have Joseph Shardin dug up, and when an autopsy was done the finding was that Shardin had committed suicide after all, but that he had, at some recent time prior to the suicide, been severely tortured.

If the Shardin murder wasn't a murder, but was a suicide, then the Younger suicide wasn't a suicide, but was a murder.

And there were other things. A shovel in Younger's office, just an ordinary shovel. But what was it doing there? Regan took to prowling around the Shardin house, and after a while he noticed where a part of the cellar had been dug up and filled in again, and when he had it dug up again there was a body in there, and it turned out to be the teenager from next door, a nineteen-year-old boy who'd supposedly left a note and gone away on a trip a few days before.

It began to seem to Regan that Charles Willis was the key to the whole thing. But Willis was gone, and so was the Samuels woman. Still, Regan wanted to talk to them.

There were fingerprints in the hotel room Willis had occupied his first night that matched up with fingerprints in the Shardin house, where Willis had lived the rest of his stay in town. It took a while to get the fingerprints and match them up, but when Regan had two good ones he sent them off to Washington to see what he could find out about Charles Willis.

Everything would have worked fine if Younger really had killed Joe Sheer, but he hadn't, and from that it just kept rolling and rolling, and finished with an answer from Washington, saying the man called Charles Willis was really Ronald Casper, wanted in California for jail-break and murder. Mug shots followed, but Parker had had plastic surgery done on his face since he'd served time as Ronald Casper, so when the mug shots didn't look like Charles Willis it slowed everybody down a little.

But not for long. Regan knew something was wrong somewhere along the line, but he didn't yet know what. He sent out another request; would the FBI office in Miami take a look for Charles Willis there? The address he'd given had probably been phoney, of course, but just to be on the safe side somebody ought to check it.

Another surprise; the address wasn't phoney after all.

9

Parker was waiting for the elevator when the manager came over and said, "Could I see you a minute? In my office."

"What's up?"

"It should be private."

Parker looked at him. The manager's name was Freedman, J. A. Freedman. Parker had spent a month or two of each of the last ten years at this hotel, and by now he knew J. A. Freedman pretty well.

Freedman touched Parker's arm and said, softly, "It's important. Really."

"All right."

Freedman led the way to his office. He was short and barrel-shaped and walked as though he'd do better if he rolled instead. His face was made of Silly Putty, plus horn-rimmed glasses.

In his office, he motioned Parker to sit down and then said, "Frankly, Mr. Willis, this is somewhat embarrassing. I don't quite know how to go about it."

"What's the problem?"

"Apparently," Freedman said, making vague gestures as though he wanted to minimize what he was saying, "apparently, you're in some sort of trouble. It's none of my business, tax trouble, I suppose, business trouble of some kind. It could happen to any of us, to me, to anybody."

It was almost two weeks since he'd come back from Sagamore. The woman he'd left down here had been gone by the time he'd come back, so he'd been keeping Rhonda around since then. As soon as Freedman said trouble, Parker knew it had to do with Sagamore, something had broken there. He said, "Why do you say I'm in trouble?"

"Two Federal agents came here looking for you."

It was Sagamore. He said, "What did they say?"

"Nothing, Mr. Willis. Only that they were looking for you."

"What did *you* say?"

Freedman spread his hands. "I have to co-operate. You're a businessman yourself, you understand the problem."

"Sure."

"I told them your room number, but that I didn't believe you were in. They said they'd wait in your room. I sent them up with a bellboy to let them in, and I've been watching for you ever since. Half an hour, I suppose. The least I can do is warn you. There are two of them, so I imagine they hope to catch you off-guard, get you to say more than you should. I thought you should know, in case you want to contact your attorney, make any preparations."

They already had Rhonda. She'd hold out five minutes when she found out they were Federal. Parker said, "Thanks. I appreciate this."

"Not at all. Our positions could easily be reversed." Freedman smiled sadly. "Government doesn't understand business," he said.

Parker got to his feet. "Things I'd better do first," he said.

"Of course, of course. I hope this trouble won't— inconvenience you too badly."

"Maybe it won't. Thanks again."

"Any time."

Parker went back out to the lobby. Did they have another man down here? Did they have pictures of him? He didn't cross the lobby, but went the other way, through the bar and out of the door on the other side and diagonally across to the hack stand. He didn't wait for the boy in the purple uniform to open the door for him, but did it himself and crowded into the back seat. "Coconut Grove," he said. "Bayshore Drive." The first address that came into his head, to get him away from here.

Riding away from the hotel, he wondered what had gone wrong. Well, it didn't matter. It had gone sour, that's all. The Charles Willis name was useless now, the whole cover shot.

It meant about sixty thousand to him, too, stashed away in bank accounts and hotel safes under the Willis name. He didn't dare go after any of that now. He had about a hundred on him, and that was it, that was all he had to get started on.

In Coconut Grove he left the cab and stole a car, a white Rambler station wagon. He pointed it north and started driving, leaving behind everything, the name he'd built up and the money he'd stashed, and the whole pattern of life he'd developed.

Already he was thinking about what to do next. He'd have to set up a new cover, but that would take a while; building it bit by bit and paper by paper till it had the texture of reality. In the meantime he had to find a place to hole up, and he had to find a score he could connect with. He was going to need cash and soon, and a lot of it.

It would work itself out. He drove north.

PARKER NOVELS BY RICHARD STARK

The Hunter [Payback]
The Man with the Getaway Face
The Outfit
The Mourner
The Score
The Jugger
The Seventh
The Handle
The Rare Coin Score
The Green Eagle Score
The Black Ice Score
The Sour Lemon Score
Deadly Edge
Slayground
Plunder Squad
Butcher's Moon
Comeback
Backflash
Flashfire
Firebreak
Breakout
Nobody Runs Forever
Ask the Parrot
Dirty Money